ACE CARROWAY
AND THE
DEADLY VIOLIN

GUY WORTHEY

ACE CARROWAY AND THE DEADLY VIOLIN

Cover design: Guy Worthey

ISBN: 1-949827-52-6
ISBN-13: 978-1-949827-52-1

Westing Press

To Diane, with love.

Ballycrispin Crier

Cork County Daily   Friday, Sept 8, 1922

MOHR'S KIN RALLY TO THE DEFENSE OF ACCUSED WIDOW

UPPER BREAHIG, Sep. 6 — A sister and brother of Dr. C. Franklin Mohr today rallied to the defense of his widow, Mrs. Morna F. Mohr, on trial for instigating his murder. After Eugene Sullivan, the woman's brother-in-law, had identified the letter offered on Saturday in which Dr. Mohr admitted the validity of his marriage, Mrs. Loughane, the doctor's sister, said that Mrs. Mohr expressed love and affection for him. Mr. Mohr, his brother, testified that Mrs. Mohr wrote to him last June asking his aid in bringing about a reconciliation with her husband about the same time the witness declared the doctor wrote him that Mrs. Mohr "was no good" and that "the children she claims are not my own." Several other witnesses testified as to matters heretofore brought out at the trial. Little of this testimony related, however, to Cillian V. Brown and Gerrit H. Spellman, who, according to the State, killed the physician and wounded his companion, Miss Emily Burger. Miss Elizabeth Darcy testified that she accompanied Mrs. Mohr to the hospital, where Dr. Mohr was taken after being shot, and that she was "grief-stricken." Winfield Thompson, a newspaperman of Lamb's Head, testified that when he asked Spellman how much money Mrs. Mohr gave him or promised him he replied,

AIRSHIP SPOTTER VINDICATED

GLOUNSHAROON. Sep. 7 — News from abroad has reversed the fortunes of ridiculed dog trainer Derry Withershins, who reported seeing an airship of the dirigible variety marked NX51 over southern Ireland in July. His description at the time caused a brief panic over fears of a renewed attack by the Ottoman Empire, followed by censure as Withershins' story could not be verified by other witnesses. But he's out of the doghouse now. Mrs. Meara O'Toole of Ballydonegan presented the Ballycrispin Crier with a stack of papers telling the whole story. The airship was entirely real, piloted by war hero Cecilia "Ace" Carroway. The exact call letters recalled by Withershins were painted upon its skin. At the time he spotted it, the craft had come nonstop from Canada and would shortly land at Croydon field outside London. From there, it flew over Europe to Egypt. While there, Carroway and her crew recovered jewels stolen from Devonshire, England. They returned the jewels and then flew back to the New World, but this time not even Derry Withershins saw them go.

The dirigible was of Carroway's invention and manufacture, and only slightly less lengthy than the Ottoman X8 she captured during the Great War. Carroway later attempted to fly solo around the world, but went missing and for many months was presumed dead.

Ace Carroway and the Deadly Violin

Chapter 1

"P. Charles Derkin!" blurted the underfed man, hands busy mangling the hat he had just removed from his head.

"How do you spell that last name?" nasally inquired the receptionist. She peered up at the supplicant over the edges of half-glasses perched on her nose and secured around her neck by a light silver chain. Mrs. Figgins ached to eject the nervous fellow. But then, Mrs. Figgins had a strong desire to send *everyone* that walked into the spotless C. Carroway and Associates office back to the dirty streets of New York from whence they came.

"D-E-R-K-I-N," the man dutifully spelled for the formidable dame behind the desk. He stopped mutilating his hat for a moment to run fingers through light brown, swept-back hair.

"Nature of the problem," droned Mrs. Figgins.

"I think I—" P. Charles Derkin swallowed convulsively. He mopped at his brow, first with his abused hat and then (after a hasty search) with a silk handkerchief. He leaned toward Mrs. Figgins's ear and resumed with a tremulous whisper. "I think I'm about to die, horribly!"

"I don't think so, sir. I'm barely even angry," Mrs. Figgins deadpanned. "Have you talked to the police?"

Derkin ground his teeth together. "The Canadian Mounties, yes. But never again. Out of the question! To my front, the police would ask about how many drinks I'd had. And behind my back, they would joke and snicker. Just like the Mounties did."

"Is there a history of insanity in your family?"

"No! The Derkins of Toronto are beyond reproach! Now, look here, miss, this is no joking matter! I'm serious."

"So are we, Mr. Derkin. As serious as they come." Mrs. Figgins's eyes flicked downward. On her desk but hidden from the client's view, a tiny electric light winked on, bright green in color. The detectives wanted an interview. Her severe expression inched more toward disapproving. Reluctantly, Mrs. Figgins forced her lips to move. "Have a seat in the lounge ..." Her jaw worked, and her sour face grew a shade more lemony. "... please. Someone will see you shortly."

Derkin was about thirty-five, of medium height, and seemed an indoors type. His proud shock of sandy brown hair flared away from a sensitive face set with blue, intelligent eyes. His suit hung loosely on his spare, almost bony frame. He stepped toward the third-floor windows overlooking Wall Street. The lounge consisted of the open space between Mrs. Figgins's array of desks and the windowed wall. Comfortable chairs circled an oval rug.

He glanced outside. Like the New Yorkers scurrying along the sidewalks, he gave no sign that he appreciated the soaring architectural marvels of the city. He was blind to the expansive blue sky dotted with roaming cloud puffballs. Instead, he perched straight-backed on the front two inches of a seat. He fidgeted with his hat, which suffered further under the aimless creasing and spindling.

The severe receptionist took up her stenographer's

pad and a freshly sharpened pencil. A second woman emerged from a door opposite the lounge, headed for Derkin. Mrs. Figgins fell into step behind her with choreography worthy of the ballet, heels clicking on the tile floor like castanets.

The new woman could have rested her chin on Mrs. Figgins's gray-sprinkled head without standing on tiptoe. Short, unruly golden hair blended with her skin tones. A simple flight suit with a wide belt clad her lithe frame.

Mrs. Figgins said, "P. Charles Derkin. Cecilia Carroway." She promptly folded into a seat and flipped to a blank page in her shorthand book.

Carroway's right eyebrow rose a millimeter. In a controlled, vibrant contralto, she said, "The concertmaster of the Toronto Symphony, unless I am mistaken. A pleasure to make your acquaintance, Mr. Derkin."

"By Corelli's cornet, what refreshing words! I suddenly feel that I'm in the right place, after all!" Derkin sent a brief sneer to Mrs. Figgins. Mrs. Figgins noticed the sneer about as much as a sea turtle notices a rainstorm. She prepared to transcribe the conversation in shorthand.

Carroway and Derkin shook hands. Four parallel slashes across the dark skin of her cheek and temple drew his attention. The scars marked her lean, decisive face with lines of dire experience. Across his face, traces of a hopeful smile tentatively flitted.

The woman in the flight suit settled into a seat. "Why don't you start at the beginning. Tell us what brought you here, Mr. Derkin."

Derkin had forgotten to be tense. "What brought

me here was a chance meeting with an old acquaint-ance at Grand Central Station. I said I was in a tizzy, and she recommended I try Carroway and Associates."

"Who was that?"

"Marilyn Murchison is her name."

Both of Carroway's eyebrows raised. "Makes sense. We managed her case[1] rather well, in the end. I had no idea she was back in town. But why don't you start further back. At the beginning."

"The beginning? Well, I suppose it was the phone call from Filbert Monocles. He said I'd inherited the Cremona Cannon."

A new male voice rolled an interjection. "Canon: a musical tune with a melody that overlaps itself." A blond fellow with a trim beard approached. A darker-haired gentleman followed, impeccably dressed in a suit with matching lapel pin, cuff links, and tie bar.

Cecilia Carroway glanced at the handsome pair. "Have a seat, Quack. Have a seat, Bert." Her golden irises flicked back to Derkin. "These are two of my associates. Fellas, this is the violinist P. Charles Der-kin."

"Hello," Derkin said.

The two newcomers settled on chairs.

Carroway glanced at the blond fellow. "Wrong sort of canon, Quack."

Bert spoke in a New England twang, "So Quack is wrong. No surprise, there."

"More than you knew, Bert." The blond's rugged face remained placid. "Not the musical canon, Ace? What, then?"

---

[1] Related in *Ace Carroway and the Growling Death*.

"The cannon in 'Cremona Cannon' is the big gun sort of cannon, but figuratively, not literally." Carroway's eyes swiveled to the violinist, where they stayed, sifting and judging. "The Cannon is a violin. A very old violin with a curious history. It comes from Cremona, the town where Antonio Stradivari had his shop, but most assume it was made either by a student or a competitor because it does not conform to the shape favored by Stradivari. Some believe that Stradivari's hands did carve it, but that it was an experimental instrument. Apparently, it never contained a maker's label. It's called a cannon because it is so loud. Its sound can easily fill a concert hall."

"A masterful summary. Brava!" said Derkin, with an emphatic nod that sent a wave through his longish, glossy hair. "But it can also be whisper quiet. It can soar in flights of romance or lightly dance to the precision required by Mozart. It can be smooth as glassy waters or brassy and bold as crashing ocean waves. The Cremona Cannon is among the very best violins in the world. And Filbert Monocles called me out of the blue and told me I had inherited it!"

Quack rolled the name off his tongue. "Who is Fillbert Mon-o-kleeze?"

Bert smirked. "Filbert Monocles translates from the Greek as 'he who eats only a single nut.'"

"Oh, haw, haw," muttered Quack blackly.

"The name is not familiar to me." Carroway studied Derkin. His clothing. His rumpled hat. His slender fingers.

The violinist's rush of words gushed like water undammed. "Filbert Monocles works for I.S.P.H.A., the International Society for the Preservation of Historical Artifacts. The Cremona Cannon had belonged to Ekaterina Brusikova. Perhaps you know her or her work. No? Well, she was the fieriest of Prussian virtuosi. Her European tour was critically acclaimed, and that was before she inherited the Cannon. But back to Mr. Monocles. He called and said that Ekaterina had passed away and that I was named the next heir to the Cremona Cannon! You can imagine my shock. Pleasure, to be sure, but also a sense of responsibility. There is only one Cremona Cannon. It is irreplaceable."

"Why were you named as heir in Ekaterina Brusikova's will?" asked dark-haired Bert. His full name was Hubert Ewing Devery Christopher Bostock III, Boston-area lawyer and noted icon of men's fashion. "It sounded as if you knew her mostly by reputation. And you're not in her family, are you?"

"No, no. I never met her in person. A couple of months ago, I did get a letter explaining that I was heir to the Cremona Cannon, but at the time, I paid no attention. Maybe 'heir' isn't quite the right word, but the process works like inheritance. The violin belongs to me as if it were on loan to me, but the ISPHA oversees the inheritance part, so I can't just dispose of it." Derkin had gained a good deal of composure by now, to the great benefit of his hat, which lay forgotten on the seat beside him. "Some three weeks after the phone call, Filbert Monocles delivered the Cannon to me. He had been travelling with the instrument from Danzig, in Prussia, to Toronto the whole time. His people wheeled it into my house."

Bert's forehead creased. "I thought violins were small and dainty."

Derkin barked a short laugh, revealing pleasant crow's feet at the corners of his eyes. "They wheeled in its safe, I mean. The instrument travels in a very heavy steel safe. Before I could even see it, I was made to fill out the paperwork. I had to name the next heir, then and there."

Bert's forehead wrinkled, and his eyebrows shot up. "Really, now? How interesting. It's similar to inheritance in the legal sense. So who is the next heir?"

"It wasn't that hard to name one." Derkin languidly gestured with a lean, long-fingered hand. "Monocles told me that it had to be a world-class violinist. One who could appreciate the Cremona Cannon and one who would play it for the pleasure of audiences. I chose young Sarah Street, that Californian you've no doubt heard of."

Bert's and Quack's faces stayed blank. Derkin's lips compressed. "Erm. Or not, as the case may be. At any rate, now I wish I hadn't. I wish I had named some political figure that should be assassinated. A pity I don't follow politics." Derkin recovered his hat and renewed his program of attempted mutilation upon the hapless felt brim. "I don't want Sarah Street to have it, because I don't wish harm upon her!"

"Harm? How?" asked Quack in confusion.

Derkin blurted out, exasperated, "It's cursed! The violin kills its owners!"

CHAPTER 2

Quack and Bert regarded each other's skeptical faces. Cecilia Carroway kept her eyes on Derkin. Mrs. Figgins dutifully scratched away on her stenography pad.

"I have evidence. I have evidence," muttered Derkin as he tried to twist his hat into a pretzel shape. "I went to the library and read some foreign papers. Ekaterina Brusikova was found impaled on a Gothic iron fence."

"Huh!" Quack's brow furrowed. "I didn't see *that* coming!"

Derkin nodded. His voice quavered. "She had jumped from an upper story window. Horrible. Gruesome. And there was a note, typed out. A suicide note. The note said the violin preyed upon her mind until she couldn't stand its voice in her head anymore."

"Spirit voices," Quack said solemnly.

Derkin's voice rose in pitch, and a flush darkened his cheeks. "There's more. I wondered who had the Cannon before Ekaterina Brusikova. I asked Monocles. He said it was Thorpe G. Scott. Ha! See?"

Quack and Bert looked owlishly uncomprehending.

Cecilia Carroway glanced at the pair. "Thorpe G. Scott was a violinist with a long solo career. He was concertmaster of the London Philharmonic for a time. His playing has recently been used to improve magnetic sound recording techniques. He was electrocuted in his bathtub some six months ago."

"Thanks, Ace." Quack bowed his head to her.

Derkin stared at Carroway. "I never expected a detective to know anything about the world of classical music."

"Ace is a lot more than just a detective." Bert flashed a roguish grin. "But we're off track. So this Scott fellow died six months ago, and then the violin went to Ekaterina Brass-whatever, and then she died and the violin came to you. Is that about right?"

Derkin sent feverish nods to Bert. "That's right, except the deaths were both freakish. And outlandish and horrifying. But I'm not done with my story. There is also what's been happening to me. Since I got the Cannon, I mean."

"Tell us all the details. No rush," Ace advised in soothing tones. Mrs. Figgins flipped to a fresh page in her stenographer's pad.

A greenish tinge stole over Derkin's skin, and he cupped his face in hands that trembled slightly. "I'll do my best. Well, first off, I'm required to keep the violin locked up in its safe whenever I'm home. ISPHA provided the safe, and I had them put it by the piano. They also sent workmen to install bigger locks on my windows and doors. Monocles said that ISPHA will send a guard to watch over it when I travel. I haven't been travelling, lately, until this New York trip."

"You live in Toronto?" Ace interjected.

"Yes, a smallish two-story house. I sleep upstairs, and the violin sits inside the safe, downstairs. At night, it—" Derkin broke off and shuddered.

Bert's face pinched. "It what?"

Derkin kept his eyes on Ace's calm visage. He drew in a shaky breath. "At night, it will sometimes make

10

noises. Creaks and groans and hollow wooden cackles. I used to enjoy a late-night glass of sherry, but now I don't. I go straight to my bedroom and talk myself to sleep."

Derkin shuddered again. "But I have to keep my eyes shut, or the ghost lights distract me. Sometimes, I see distorted violin shapes in different colors. Other times, there will be flashes like lightning, but outside there are no storms. If I get up to look, there is nothing to see. I dream of it, now. Dreams in which a violin laughs madly and reaches out its strings to garrote me. Or dreams in which I run and run and run, but I can't get away from the beautiful sound of the violin, even though I know if I hear it too long, the sound will drag me beneath the earth to die."

Derkin's voice rose, and sweat gleamed on his face. He rubbed long-fingered, palsied hands over his shiny brow. "I ... I forgot to mention the winds. There are winds, sometimes, moaning and rushing. Even when it is calm out. And it's all happened since I got the violin."

Quack lifted a finger to stroke the blond fuzz on his upper lip.

The slight motion seemed to irritate Derkin and put him on the defensive. He addressed Quack, a touch of anger sharpening his words. "I nearly died two days ago! My car brakes went out. I was heading to the beach at Bluffer's Park, and they quit as I came down Brimley. If I had been further up the hill, I would probably be dead now. As it was, I was near enough to the bottom to get more or less on the flat. I steered off the road. I obliterated a gentleman's hedge, but it stopped the car."

Derkin spread his hands and regarded each face in turn. "You see now? I'm cursed. I want this investigated, and I don't want the Mounties giving me lip service and then laughing at me as soon as my back is turned!" He spoke with verve, but a moment later, his flash of resolve evaporated. He whimpered and snatched up his mangled hat, wringing the once-crisp felt cruelly.

Quack and Bert cast sympathetic eyes upon the sweat-sheened fellow, but Ace powered ahead. "What new people have come to your door since you received the violin?"

"Well, Filbert Monocles. And two large fellows that he had with him to wheel the safe around. And a locksmith to improve my doors," Derkin said, surprised out of his funk. "Oh, and Miss Rosavino, of course."

"Who is Miss Rosavino?"

"A photographer. She wants to photograph me with the Cremona Cannon. And also take pictures and measurements of the instrument itself for scientific purposes. We haven't been able to arrange all that yet."

"Anyone else? Any phone calls from strangers?"

"I ... I don't recall."

"Jot down a list when you do. It could be vital. Note phone calls from everyone, family, friend, or stranger."

"Oh. All right. So, does that mean you'll take the case?"

"It does."

Business clicked along rapidly after that. Mrs. Figgins ensured the contract for investigation was properly signed and accepted a cheque as initial payment. Ace promised to meet P. Charles Derkin at his Toronto home the following afternoon. Carroway, Bert, and

Quack said farewell to Derkin, and he exited down the stairwell.

The three eased back down in the lounge seats to mull things over. Mrs. Figgins clacked on her typewriter.

Ace steepled her fingers. "Quack, did you notice any psychological inconsistencies?"

Quack wagged his blond head in the negative. "It's hard to fake an attack of nerves like that. The man's scared, pure and simple."

Bert gritted his teeth. "I don't like the ghosts angle, and I don't believe in curses."

"And yet," Quack said in an ominous basso, "the violin seems to have a lot of blood on its strings."

"We're at the beginning of the case, there's a lot to be—" Ace broke off. A brief shadow darkened the window. A mere eye blink, but Ace's acute senses detected motion. Swift downward motion.

Ace leapt off her chair. "Come on!" A golden blur, she streaked to the exit. She banged through the door lettered "C. Carroway and Associates" before Bert and Quack could do more than twitch. Belatedly, they pelted along after, hurtling down the stairs to the building lobby and then outside.

On the sidewalk, citizens gathered in a loose circle around a downed P. Charles Derkin. He sprawled on his back, feet pointing toward a shattered concrete rubble pile on the pavement. Some of the fragments looked squared off, like parts of a common cinder block.

Bert and Quack pushed through the people.

Ace hovered over Derkin's prone form, checking his pupil dilation and pulse. No blood was evident.

Indeed, except for the pasty hue of his skin, the violinist appeared undamaged. He stared skyward and listlessly muttered, "Almost got me, that time. Almost. Almost killed. Killed dead."

CHAPTER 3

Ace glanced up to Bert and Quack. "Get around back. To the fire escape. Run!"

The men did not hesitate. They sprinted down Wall Street and tore into the alley. A small motor revved.

"Motorcycle, sounds like!" breathlessly puffed Quack. The two men ran neck and neck down the alley, weaving around trash bins and railings.

"There!" Bert stabbed a finger straight ahead.

A motorcycle sped straight toward them. The rider's face was hidden behind large goggles, but it appeared to be a clean-shaven man. Upon seeing Bert and Quack, the rider spun his motorcycle around in a cloud of rubber smoke and accelerated the opposite way.

"Hey!" Quack gasped. He poured on a burst of speed, but his grabbing fingers missed the taillight. The motorcycle sped away and spat gravel back into Quack's face.

The two-wheeler screeched around the next bend in the alley and headed for Broadway as the men ran after. It popped out into the street, heedless of pedestrians and reckless of traffic. Moments too late to intercept it, a flight-suited figure skidded to a halt in the alley entrance. Ace didn't give chase. She rested her hands on her hips and stared after the speeding machine. Quack and Bert joined her and put their hands on their knees to huff and blow.

Ace rattled off in precise tones, "Bert, that was a Scott Flying Squirrel, last year's model. No license plate. Take the Roadster and go ask that motorcycle dealer down Broadway about eight blocks if somebody rented one recently. If so, get his description."

"Yeah. Can do, Ace!" said Bert, holding his side.

"Quack, climb the fire escape. See if you can spot clues up there. I'll get Derkin back on his feet. Meet back at the agency."

"Sure thing, Ace!" Quack said with a grin.

They split up and went their separate ways. All three were happy as dogs at dinnertime due to a very simple fact: the action had started.

Bert was the last to join the conference. Typing sounds from Mrs. Figgins provided background ambiance, albeit not the same quality as Chopin or Saint-Saens. Bert plopped into a seat and enthused, "Good guess, Ace. That dealer you remembered was where the motorcycle came from."

"Did you get a physical description?" Ace asked.

Bert's face twisted into a dubious squint. "Not a great one. Medium height, medium build, Caucasian, hazel eyes, no spectacles. English accent. The accent might narrow it down a little bit. He paid in cash. I told 'em to give us a call if by chance the motorcycle gets returned. Oh, and he gave the name of John Smith."

Quack shook his head from side to side. "John Smith. Really, now? Not very original."

Bert shrugged his shoulders. "What about you,

Quack? Did you find anything?"

The blonder gentleman puffed air through his nose. "A stack of cinder blocks is piled near the fire escape. That's all I saw."

"And P. Charles Derkin?" asked Bert.

Ace replied, "Well, I wouldn't take any bets on his state of mind, but his body is resting in a local hotel. He has a concert tonight, here in New York."

Quack pursed his lips. "He hired detectives and will give a concert, too. Busy man."

"Nervous man." Bert straightened his tie, unnecessarily. "How could he treat a perfectly good hat that way?"

"He was hat-hazard." Ace grinned big.

Bert and Quack grew pained expressions.

Ace's grin faded. She cleared her throat. "I'm thinking we should shadow him. Today's tossed cinder block removes any doubt that real danger exists. I hope we can get to the bottom of the mystery before the mystery puts Mr. Derkin six feet under."

"You think it's that deadly, Ace?" Quack said.

"I think Mr. Derkin is quite possibly expendable compared to the violin. It's the violin that's precious. And, yes, something about that violin is lethal."

They exchanged sober glances. Ace continued briskly, "I'm going to telegram Sam. He's not too far from Danzig, where Ekaterina Brusikova met her grisly end. Maybe he can poke around for facts."

"Oh, right. He and Gooper[2] got interested in insect farms. In Prussia." Bert shook his head in wonder-

---

[2] Sam Raia Biming and Phileas "Gooper" Locknard are associates of Ace Carroway.

17

ment. "They're such hopeless eggheads."

Quack pursed his lips. "No, I thought they were after some kind of early human archaeology."

"Both, as I recall," Ace said. "Gentlemen? Find your tuxedos. We're stepping out tonight."

Chapter 4

Hours ahead of curtain call, Ace, Bert, and Quack escorted P. Charles Derkin to the concert hall. The Baroque Theater was furnished in wood panels with carved frames, plush carpets, marble staircases with brass railings, and stone columns decorated with ornate filigree and gargoyles. In better light, it might be called elegant, but the flickering gloom of its gas lamps cloaked it in ominous shadows.

All three gentlemen wore tuxedos, and Derkin's coat had tails. Ace wore a slim, black dress whose simplicity was offset by a bold black-and-white triangular collar. A beret sat at an angle on her head, and she had tamed her unruly crop of golden hair to glossy waves.

Quack emitted a long whistle. "That's a new look for you, Ace! It's spectacular!"

"Flight suits are out. I need to blend in," Ace rationalized.

"Ace Carroway blending in?" Bert grew a grin. "That's categorically impossible."

"Oh?" Ace's face fell.

Quack soothed, "In the best of ways, Ace, you stand out in a crowd."

Bert and Quack led the hunt for the manager. They found her in the box office. The harried middle-aged woman proved susceptible to their double dose of dapper. She drafted them as ushers for the evening, and on the strength of Charles Derkin's word, Ace won full backstage privileges.

Derkin and Ace wound their way past the rows of seats to the stage, to the right of which hid a backstage door. At the entrance to the row of dressing rooms, a slender man in a suit and a cane sat motionless. With hands folded over the curve of his cane handle, he held himself straight-backed on a folding chair and stared forward. When he detected the approach of Derkin and Ace, he pushed to his feet and fished a disk of glass connected to a chain out of his vest pocket. He wedged the optic into his eye orbit and examined the pair.

Derkin said glumly, "Miss Carroway, may I present Filbert Monocles. Mr. Monocles, this is Cecilia Carroway."

"A pleasure, Miss Carroway. Are you a photographer, too?" The small, bony man squinted upwards at the tall woman. His voice sounded like a buzzing wasp, tense and awake.

"Why, no. Is my vocation relevant?" Ace did not smile.

"No, no. Pardon me. The other one is a photographer, that's all," Monocles said.

Storms brewed in Ace's eyes. "The other *what*, exactly?"

Derkin's vexed eyebrows knit together. "Mr. Monocles, just unlock the violin, if you please."

Previously part of the antique ambiance of the decor, a hulking metal safe next to Monocles suddenly gained new significance. The wispy-haired little man bowed curtly to Derkin and bent to twirl the tumblers.

Derkin glanced at Ace and rubbed the back of his

neck. "There is a Miss Isabella Rosavino who is a photographer. She should soon be——"

"Here, darling!" sang out a female voice from the direction of the stage.

"Yes, here. To take photographs." P. Charles Derkin ran a hand through his dramatic hair. His lips curved upward. "Isa, this is Miss Cecilia Carroway. Miss Carroway, this is Miss Isabella Rosavino."

A trim young woman flew to Derkin, took his hands, and pecked his right cheek, then his left. The hem of her burgundy dress swished six inches above her ankles as dictated by the current year's fashion. She wore vivid red lipstick, but her lashes, eyebrows, and curly tresses gleamed black. Jaunty traces of perfume enlivened the otherwise musky backstage air.

Filbert Monocles levered the safe latch and swung its silent door open. He inserted his arms into its recess and tenderly withdrew a violin case.

Ace and Isabella clasped hands and repeated the cheek kissing ritual. The shapely photographer spoke with lilting Italian accents, "A pleasure, Cecilia. Are you a fan of Mr. Derkin's? Perhaps he has many admirers."

Ace shook her head. "I'm in his employ. This will be the first time I have heard him in concert."

Isa's eyes flashed wide. "Your ears, they will taste a delectable feast."

The photographer carried a bag bulging with camera accessories. Ace attempted to surreptitiously study the raven-haired woman, but Isa caught her looking. Boldly, the Italian swept her eyes up and down Ace from hair to heels.

Derkin accepted the violin case from Filbert Monocles, but the official raised a finger to catch his attention. "Mr. Derkin, a moment of your time, please. I am due to depart for Copenhagen this evening. By now, you should be comfortable with the security procedures regarding the Cremona Cannon. I leave you in the capable hands of the Continental Assurance Company. They can provide security throughout the United States and Canada."

"You are leaving? I see." P. Charles Derkin sounded both relieved and apprehensive. "What if I travel abroad?"

"Simply send a wire to ISPHA-Copenhagen. We will make it as easy as possible on you, Mr. Derkin." greasily buzzed Filbert Monocles. A small smile tightened the skin around his monocle for a moment.

Derkin held the violin case to his chest. "Yes, all right."

"I regret not hearing you play the Cannon this evening, Mr. Derkin, but it has been a privilege to meet you. The Cremona Cannon has found an excellent home with you. You play with all the fire and ice, feathers and steel, ecstasy and agony that Ekaterina Brusikova did, may she rest in peace."

Ace thought Filbert Monocles sounded sincere. Isabella Rosavino sidled up to slip a hand into the crook of Derkin's elbow.

P. Charles Derkin's voice gained a noticeable quaver. "Y-yes. Rest in peace. Thank you, Mr. Monocles. Have a safe journey."

Filbert Monocles removed the lens from his eye and stowed it in his vest pocket. He bowed crisply and cane-clicked his way out.

"You are very brave, Charles, to take the violin that

has caused so much—" Isabella locked eyes with Derkin. "—death."

"D-death! Oh, help!" Derkin's gaze snapped down to the violin case in his hand.

"Oh, don't worry, darling. My own family, the Rosavinos, we have a ghost. Yes, yes. A different part of Italy than Cremona, but a ghost like the one that haunts this violin. The secret is to laugh! Ha, ha! See? No ghost can harm you when you laugh." Isabella squeezed Derkin's elbow for emphasis.

"So your ghost doesn't kill people," said Derkin.

"That I did *not* say. An ancestor of mine was a smith. It is said he treated his apprentice badly and one day beat him to death with a smith's hammer. This story is no compliment to my family. Such shame, to have a murderer for an ancestor, yes?"

Derkin hooked a finger under his collar and tugged. "I, uh, I wouldn't know, firsthand."

"Lucky you, Charles. Soon after this bloody killing, the smith was himself found dead in his smithy. His head was cracked open, like an egg is cracked for breakfast." Isabella gestured with both hands, miming a head splitting apart. Derkin cringed.

Isabella's eyes roved from face to face. "Some say that the ghost of the apprentice took a hammer in his spectral hand. Up it raised and down it fell and the apprentice made his bloody revenge."

Her voice hushed. Even Ace leaned closer to the narrator to hear her story. "Ever after, in my house, sometimes we hear hammer sounds at night. Sometimes in the morning, we find marks on the door like someone had smashed a square-faced hammer there. Sometimes, windows will shatter."

At the word "shatter," a boom shook the air and echoed in the backstage hall and theater. It sounded like a piano falling over or a heavy door slamming.

P. Charles Derkin jerked in a spasm of fright. "Ahh!"

Isabella chimed in. "Aiieeee!"

Ace was in motion, running toward the sound. Before completing one step, she found her legs could not run, due to her sheath dress. "Oh, cripes!" She shuffled as fast as she could, feeling ridiculous. As she entered the theater itself, she caught a glimpse of something brown by the lobby exit. The impression was fleeting. On second glance, all was still.

Quack and Bert popped through a lobby door and loped down the side aisle. Catching sight of Ace, they jogged over. "What was that boom?"

Ace planted fists on her hips and gazed around at the quiet rows of seats. "I don't know. Coincidence, perhaps."

Isabella Rosavino frisked into view, dragging a pale P. Charles Derkin along behind. "Maybe the theater has a ghost, too!" she piped.

"Oo!" Quack said, eyebrows lifting at the sight of Isabella.

"Oh, my!" Bert added, equally transfixed.

Chapter 5

Other musicians arrived. A stagehand in coveralls arranged eight chairs and eight music stands around a harpsichord on stage. P. Charles Derkin opened his case and removed a violin.

Bert's eyes could not detect anything extraordinary about the instrument. His forehead wrinkled. "That's the famous violin?"

Derkin sent him a superior smirk. "Wait until you hear it."

He tuned the honey brown instrument and began to play scales to warm up his fingers. Even at these first hints, the ear perked up. When Derkin pulled his bow across the strings, the sound vibrated to the corners of the room in a way that demanded attention.

Ace and her associates lined up to listen and see. Derkin's lips curled in a fatalistic grimace. "Even now, you hear it, don't you? You begin to see what a fine instrument this is. What price would you set upon it?" Derkin settled the violin under his chin and effortlessly played a scale and a trill from Vivaldi's "Winter." The notes tingled up and down the spines of the listeners. Derkin said, "I would pay anything, myself. Anything short of death. Unfortunately, death seems to be the price."

"Now, now, Mr. Derkin, let's keep our feet on the ground," Quack soothed.

A short rehearsal followed, during which Rosavino flashed photos and Bert and Quack kept eyes on

Rosavino. Musically, the Cremona Cannon soared over the accompaniment. Its expressive voice spoke with crystalline clarity and sang with haunting beauty.

At the appointed hour, word passed from mouth to mouth backstage. "House is open!" Quack and Bert ushered audience members to their seats while Ace kept backstage. Try as she might, however, she could not be inconspicuous. To the detriment of her body-guard role, one cellist in particular began staring at her. The fellow never worked up the courage to speak, but he followed her if she happened to roam out of his line of sight.

Besides the musicians, a stagehand in black lounged near the stage. A custodian in drab coveralls attempted to snooze while leaning on a broom. Isabella Rosavino hovered backstage near Derkin, but the violinist shooed her out to the house with palsied fingers.

The first composition, a collection of dances by Gabrieli, Derkin did not join. He sat in silence, sway-ing to inner music, the Cremona Cannon held loosely in one hand. As the first piece wrapped up, the stage-hand beckoned to Derkin, who nodded, took a shaky breath, and went off to the stage. There was more ap-plause, and the Tartini violin concerto began. Ace stayed backstage, keeping vigil.

The custodian shuffled by. He gave Ace a grin and remarked in a Georgia drawl, "Nice, quiet evenin', eh, miss? I like a quiet crowd." Ace noticed a small gap between his top front teeth. Youthful, unkempt blond hair covered his forehead.

"A lovely evening, yes," Ace said.

The custodian shuffled on.

The Tartini ended with vigorous applause. Derkin

and the musicians flooded backstage. Abuzz with chatter, they clustered around the water pitcher. Isabella Rosavino appeared in a swish of fabric and subtle gust of perfume. She claimed Derkin's elbow. Leaning against him, she gushed praise.

Face wreathed in smiles, Derkin appeared happy and relaxed instead of nervous. Casually, he handed the Cremona Cannon and his bow to Isabella and headed to the water closet. Ace blinked and frowned. Unsure, Isabella held the priceless instrument awkwardly. Then she ducked into a dressing room, out of elbow-jostling range of the other musicians.

That put her and the Cannon out of sight of Ace, whose frown deepened. The flyer decided to chase after the famous violin, but a wide-eyed young cellist minced into her path. "Are you, um, are you Cecilia C-Carroway?"

There seemed no escape from his pleading eyes. "Yes, that's right," she said.

"I knew it!" He thrust a concert program and a pen toward her. "Could I have an autograph?"

Ace glanced to the dressing-room door. No sign of Rosavino or the Cannon. She turned a vexed expression upon the cellist. "All right." She snatched his program and scribbled her signature on it.

"I heard your Chopin performance last October. Amazing. Truly amazing."

"Glad you liked it."

He reverently received his program and pen back. "Liked it? I cried, I cheered. I'll never forget it. I scoured the papers for more concerts, but I don't think you have given any more."

"No." She could not possibly explain that the reason involved a black market dead-or-alive bounty on her head. Ace held up a finger. "Would you excuse me a moment?"

The cellist's face drooped. "Oh. All right. Thanks for the autograph, Miss Carroway."

Ace attempted a smile, then shouldered past the musician.

And there was Derkin accepting his violin from Isabella Rosavino's hands. He all but oozed confidence. Even his hair seemed to feather taller. The stagehand bawled, "Five minutes!"

The musicians filed back onstage, and Rosavino slipped away to her seat in the hall. Soon, the chill wind and icicles of Vivaldi's "Winter" drifted backstage.

Ace relaxed.

Ace relaxed too soon.

A loud, wooden bang rang out.

P. Charles Derkin's voice rose in panic, "Ahh!"

The audience in the house gasped like a gust of wind sweeping into a pine forest.

The accompaniment awkwardly trailed to silence, and out in the house, a buzz of conversation began.

Ace hiked up her skirt and ran toward the stage. She nearly collided with Derkin as he pelted offstage.

Instantly, Ace saw the issue. All the strings trailed off the violin in a curly, bouncy tangle, ending in a dangling black triangle tailpiece. The chaotic mess converged at the tuning pegs.

"It tried to kill me! It wants to kill me!" gibbered the violinist, thrusting the instrument at Ace.

Ace backed up, a glint sparking in her golden eyes. She growled, "Snap out of it, Derkin! The tailgut broke. See?" Ace held up the black triangle of the ebony tailpiece for him to examine. The loop of tough fiber that had held the tailpiece on the violin's end button was no longer a closed loop but a frayed hook.

Derkin trembled and stared wild-eyed at Ace. He covered his face with his hands. He nodded, mumbling through his fingers, "Yes, yes. I know. But tailguts don't fail every day! It's very rare. Rare. But it happened to me, tonight! I can't take it anymore!"

Ace had no sympathy for Derkin as she examined the violin. Without strings, tailpiece, and bridge, its beautiful wood grain and graceful shape stood unaltered. The instrument was undamaged despite the spectacular explosion caused by the tailgut failure. "When is your next concert?"

"T-Toronto Symphony. Next weekend." Derkin slid shaky hands off his face and peered blearily at Ace, pale and panting.

"To replace the tailgut takes a few minutes at a violin shop. You'll have the violin back in plenty of time."

"If I live that long!"

Chapter 6

At next day's breakfast, Derkin was still frantic. His sail-like wave of hair bobbed as he gestured with a forkful of scrambled egg. "I don't want to go home! I slept well in the hotel room, with the Cannon in the hotel safe. But back in Toronto, the winds will start again, and the noises, and the ghostly lights, and the dreams." He grimaced. "Such dreams!"

Derkin, Ace, Quack, and Bert sat around a table in the restaurant of Derkin's hotel. With brows knit and eyes narrowed, Bert sent a vexed glance at Derkin. Ace reposed, placid as a mountain lake. In moments like these, none could guess what might be passing through the skilled young woman's mind. Perhaps she attended to the moment and paid attention to the conversation. Perhaps her mind raced, wrapped up in one of her many inventive pursuits. Perhaps she swam through rivers of memory. The mystery of Ace Carroway herself might be a puzzle unsolvable.

Quack snapped his fingers. "Say! I've got an idea!"

Bert sniffed with aristocratic condescension. "No. Categorically, no. Whatever it is."

For once, Quack didn't rise to Bert's bait. Without so much as a facial tic, he continued, gesturing with excitement. "I could impersonate Derkin here. I'd go to his house. Sleep in his bed. I'll see the lights and hear the sounds myself."

The left side of Ace's mouth lifted in a lopsided

smile. "I'm listening."

P. Charles Derkin laid his fork down and pursed his lips. "Well, *I* like the idea."

Bert grumped, "Actor! Stealing the spotlight again."

Quack stuck his tongue out at Bert, then tapped his temple with a forefinger. "I'm about Derkin's size. I'd barely need a disguise. Just a wig so my silhouette cuts the right shape." Quack took a self-congratulatory sip of orange juice.

Ace's eyes drooped to half lidded. "We have a camera back at the lab[3], and a new Western Electric spindle sound recorder."

Bert abruptly switched sides. "Oh! And we have those little two-way radios. We could set up a surveillance blind near Derkin's house. Out of sight but ready to pounce if need be."

P. Charles Derkin said solemnly, "I do appreciate this. You three are my anchor to sanity, I swear."

The journey to Toronto proceeded without event. Carroway and her associates tossed electric gear in the trunk of the big roadster. The broken Cremona Cannon rode between Derkin and Quack in the back seat.

Upon arrival in the lakeside city, their first stop was Derkin's favorite violin repair shop, awash with the smells of wood, varnish, and rosin. The pair of crafts-

---

[3] The floor above the office where Mrs. Figgins reigns supreme is Ace's library, laboratory, and equipment locker.

men working there grew wide eyes when they realized who and what had strolled through their door. They shooed a customer out and locked the front door, and then they lovingly reassembled the violin.

They insisted on polishing the instrument and adjusting the sound post. They doted upon Derkin as he played scales and concerto excerpts between adjustments.

Quack missed most of the Cannon-worship because he left the shop to hunt for wigs. Before the sound post had been reset, he returned with a smug aspect painted upon his face. Ace and Bert absorbed the woody ambiance of the shop, learning scraps of violin lore from the giddy shopkeepers.

Quack bought a spare violin case before they left the clingy embrace of the violin shop. Their next stop was a nondescript hotel well away from city center.

As they drove, Quack hid Derkin's flamboyant hair under a fedora. The actor advised the violinist, "When you check in, use an assumed name."

Derkin seemed tickled at all the subterfuge. He embraced the spy routine with glee. "It's like a Chicago gangster story. I've even got a tommy gun!" He patted the case of the Cremona Cannon.

Because Derkin had taken the train from Toronto to New York, it stood to reason that he might be expected to return by the same method. Accordingly, they left Derkin at the hotel and drove to the train station. Quack disguised himself on the way, donning a wig that mimicked Derkin's swept-back wavy coiffure.

Bert grumbled, "You're really loving this, aren't you?"

Quack checked his appearance in the rear-view mir-

ror. "Bert, you're positively radiant when you're con-
sumed with childish envy."

"Showboat."

"Chowder-head."

"Hack."

"Leech."

"Fellas," Ace interrupted, "here's the train station.
Talk to you shortly, Quack. Good luck."

The actor saluted and slipped out of the roadster.
He carried a suitcase and his recently purchased violin
case. Collar up and with the hunched shoulders of a
weary businessman, he melted into the crowd.

Quack lurked in the shadows of the station interior
until a train from New York arrived. Now proudly
erect with his Derkin-like wig held high, he joined the
stream of travelers. He hailed a Front Street cab. Cradling his faux violin case on his lap, he gave the cabbie
Derkin's address.

As far as Quack could tell, no one followed them.
"But you can't be too careful," he muttered to himself.

"Eh?" said the cabbie, a chubby fellow who chewed
on an unlit cigar.

"My father," replied Quack, emulating Derkin's vo-
cal tones, "always said you can't be too careful. Good
advice, I say."

"Oh. Sure, sure." The cabbie rolled his eyes.

The cab swerved into a gravel driveway, and Quack
gazed out the window. The modest residence stood
two stories tall, decorated with some antique stonework at the corners. The expansive yard was enclosed
by a knee-high stone wall. The driveway wound
through trees, shrubs, and hillocks that were the crea-
tions of past gardeners. Pleasant though the view was,

Quack saw the artful landscaping with a more suspicious eye. All the obstacles made a hundred excellent hiding places.

Quack emerged from the cab, holding on to his violin case as if it were precious. He paid the driver, then opened the front door using Derkin's key. He didn't fumble it, thankfully. The cab drove off. The actor shut the front door and locked himself in.

"Well, so far, so good," he said as he scanned the spare but homey interior of the house. "Though, if it turns out there *isn't* a conspiracy, we'll all feel terribly foolish!"

He began to assemble his equipment. The camera and sound recorder resided in his suitcase, and the violin case contained a portable two-way radio.

"I wish I could scout the grounds," Ace murmured in hushed tones. "There might be clues."

"The light's fading, anyway, now." Bert, too, kept his voice well below the ambient sounds of distant traffic, birds, and the whisperings of a fitful breeze through tree branches. "So, what's the plan? Stick together and watch and wait? Or split up and watch and wait?"

They had found a large spruce tree with drooping branches at the corner of the Derkin residence lot. They burrowed into the branches, then patiently snapped off all the dead ones close to the trunk. That created a tent-like nest to inhabit, pine scented and dry. As desired, they could see fairly well by poking their heads toward gaps in the droopy branches.

"Those two upper windows mark the master bedroom," Ace mused. "I think this is a good spot for a stakeout. Let's warm up the radio."

But they were interrupted. Crunches of gravel and the whir of a motor announced the arrival of a car. A neat little two-door red Alpha Romero rolled to a stop by the front door. A woman emerged. She removed a pair of dark glasses from her eyes and resettled them into her abundant black hair.

"Isabella Rosavino," Ace said.

"Mmm, I appreciate fiery Italians," Bert murmured back.

Isabella rang the doorbell.

"What's Quack going to do?" Bert chewed on his lower lip.

"He hasn't turned on any lights yet. He'll pretend nobody's home."

Bert's handsome face frowned, then lit up in a delighted smile. "Oh, I love this. A beautiful woman comes knocking, and Quack is forced to ignore her."

"Charles?" Isabella called. Her voice carried clearly to the watchers. "Charles?"

But no one answered. A few minutes later, Isabella slipped back in her little red car and drove away.

Ace watched her go, then resumed fussing with the portable radio, inserting an earplug in her ear. She squeezed the talk lever, holding the transceiver next to her mouth. "Quack, you there?"

"Here, Ace! Tell you what, I wish I was P. Charles Derkin. That Miss Rosavino is—"

"Quack. Did you set up the gear? Over."

"Sorry, what was that, Ace? I was talking. Uh, over."

"Did you set up the gear? Over."

"Oh, oh, yes. Derkin said the violin makes funny noises, so I found the safe where he stores it. It's downstairs in the music room. I put the spindle recorder there. I'll start it at bedtime. Uh. Over."

"All right. Save the radio battery until it's dark. We're in position. Over and out."

Ace glanced at Bert. "Did you hear that?"

"Barely, yes. What a nincompoop. At least he's easily amused. Give him a wig to wear and he's happy for days."

Night fell. Crickets sang as the air grew chilly. Quack turned on some lights in the house and occasionally made his silhouette visible in the windows. Bert and Ace were impressed with the realism of his shadow. Every spy watching, if any, could see P. Charles Derkin at home, preparing for bed.

Quack flipped the lights out. A crescent moon slipped through scudding clouds. Gradually, it set in the west.

Bert blew in his hands, then clapped them to his ears. He whispered, "Is it below freezing? I can't feel my ears."

Ace had donned her leather flight cap and a scarf to go with her belted flight suit. She lounged comfortably, occasionally jamming her hands in pockets to keep them warm. Her alto voice teased, "Your ears are still attached. Why are you wearing a fancy suit to go spying in?"

"Fashion overrules comfort."

Ace's forehead scrunched up. "Err."

Bert hastily added, "Besides, I wasn't complaining!"

"Oh. You weren't complaining. My mistake. Wait! Quack's on the line."

Bert hunkered near and leaned his cold ear next to Ace's leather-covered one to eavesdrop.

Quack's hoarse whisper faintly hissed, "Listen to this!"

Even through the tinny, crackly earpiece, the sound was eerie. It was a tortured moaning, echoing metallically. Clanks and unearthly screeches punctuated the agonized keening.

The unnerving sounds faded out. Quack whispered over the radio, "Every hair on my head is standing on end. I've got nothing but sympathy for Derkin, after hearing that."

Bert and Ace expected the actor to say "Over," but instead Quack yelled, "Aah!"

With a click, the panicked sound quit, and the hiss of Quack's radio channel cut. Abrupt silence fell.

CHAPTER 7

Bert and Ace caught a flash of light somewhere beyond the lace of pine branches. They jerked their heads to track it so fast they almost gave themselves whiplash. The ghostly flicker ended, gone too soon for them to locate it with surety.

They rose to crouch positions, careful to remain silent. They pushed their faces through the tree branches toward the house, eyes straining.

There! A fleeting impression of a jagged blotch of light outlined the upstairs house windows. But a moment later, darkness reigned.

Bert growled under his breath. "What's going on?"

Ace triggered the radio. "Quack, respond. Over."

Bert pulled a spruce branch aside and pointed, down at ground level. Ace followed the pointing finger.

Shadowy movement!

In unspoken accord, they both pushed forward. They slipped past the spiny curtain of branches, keeping low. Ace tried one more time, "Quack. Respond. Over." The channel remained dead. She dropped the transmitter into a pocket for safekeeping.

There was another flash of light. Because their eyes were on the moving shadow, they caught a brief impression of a human silhouette by a bush. It held a tube on its shoulder.

A new sound began. A rushing of wind. The whoosh noise came from nearer the house. It was as if a local hurricane had whipped up, but there was no movement of air.

Free of the tree, Bert and Ace crept toward the human shadow.

Bert trod on a stick. It broke with a snap.

Ace and Bert froze. For a second, nothing happened.

A flash of brilliant white light stabbed into their eyes painfully. They caught only the vaguest impression of a human figure past the sunlike radiance.

The light cut off. A male voice barked, "Code zed!"

Ace dived forward, ending in a roll. Finding her feet again, she lunged for the voice. Afterimages danced in her vision, blocking out all sight. With hands outstretched, she hoped for the best.

Something hard struck her alongside the head accompanied by the sound of shattering glass. Stars of pain shocked her optic nerves. Ace tumbled to the ground, too dazed to control her descent.

"Another one," muttered the male voice. There was another crash of metal and glass. Bert grunted, and a body hit the ground. The windstorm-that-wasn't faded out gradually.

In addition to the airy whoosh and a sullen moan of pain from Bert, footsteps chuffed. Two sets, Ace thought, both at a full run and rapidly getting fainter. Ace struggled to her feet, blinking rapidly, trying to see something besides blotchy afterimages. She ran drunkenly toward the sound of the disappearing footsteps.

That was a rash idea. In a few steps, Ace floundered into a bush. Struggling past that obstacle, the ground fell out from in front of her as she unknowingly stepped over a low decorative terrace. She flopped forward on her face.

A new light clicked on.

Ace rolled and blearily squinted at it. She exhaled in relief. It was only the porch light over the front door.

Quack's voice rolled across the lawn. "Ace? You're not usually one to lie down on the job."

Bert's voice moaned from several yards away. "They got away, didn't they?"

In the mid-distance, an engine roared. Tires squealed. The engine sound receded.

Ace levered herself up to a sitting position. "They got away."

Quack said, "They?"

Bert said, "Ow. I think I'm bleeding. I owe somebody a knuckle sandwich."

Ace smeared garden dirt around her face with her flight suit sleeve. "Let's look around."

By the light of miniature electric torches, they tracked footsteps through the gardens and grass. The torches were but one example of the plethora of equipment adopted by Carroway and Associates. Sometimes outright inventions, sometimes a slight modification on a dime store item, Ace loved to have the right tool for the job at hand.

Quack said sheepishly, "I'm sorry. When the skeleton images flashed into the bedroom, I dropped the radio. It broke."

Bert stroked his cut and bruised jaw. "Well, you sure gave us a turn. Glad you're all right, Quack."

"Thanks," Quack replied cautiously as he cast a suspicion-filled glance at the lawyer.

Bert blinked and scowled. "No, cancel that. I meant how could you be such a milquetoast, you blockhead?"

Quack's clouded expression cleared. Sunnily, he replied, "Like you could even operate a radio, shyster."

"Fumbler."

"Me, a fumbler? Let's recap your score. Skulking goons one, Bert zero."

Ace led the way, tracking. Even as the men argued, they crossed a low wall. They left the grounds of the house and headed across the next-door neighbor's yard at a diagonal.

"Wires. See?" Ace pointed out. A shallowly buried pair of twisted wires erupted from the ground, vaulted the low wall, then reburied themselves on the far side.

"Eh? What does that mean?" Quack wondered.

Ace said nothing, continuing on at a diagonal until they reached the street.

She played her light around, then zeroed in on a spot. "There. Terminals."

The wires reappeared, ending in copper loops.

"And what does *that* mean?" Quack wondered anew.

Bert scratched his head. "Wires at the street. Hey, are there—?" Ace was a few steps further, playing her light on fresh rubber stains on the street. "Heh, yeah, there *are* peel-out marks. So a car or truck was parked here. It hooked up to these wires."

Quack whistled, low and long. "Which head straight toward the Derkin house. Well, well. The ghosts are electric."

"Let's see what hit us, Bert," Ace said.

Back in the yard, there was a broken-up metal tube. Ace prodded it with a finger. "Battery here. A big capacitor to store up charge here. Trigger. Light bulb, now broken. Lenses, now broken. Ah, slides. Here are your skeletons, Quack." Ace handed most of a broken flat glass plate to Quack. In miniature, there were images of ghastly dancing skeletons on the film.

Quack shook his blond head with slow gravity. "Whoever thought of this could be the toast of Broadway stage lighting."

Bert had wandered toward the house. "And here's a wind machine."

Eyes swiveled to where Bert's light played. Quack whistled in appreciation. "Yes, wind machine is the technical name. Any theater that ever did Mozart's *The Magic Flute* has one lurking in their storage rooms."

The device consisted of a light wooden drum with a handle attached to the axis. A drape of canvas lay over the top. Bert bent and cranked the handle. In short order, a realistic wind sound emerged.

Quack said, "That leaves only the sound of moaning and clanking to be explained."

Ace planted fists on her hips. "We shall see if we can find it. My guess is that there will be a loudspeaker inside the house hooked to those wires that trail off to the road. The truck parked there would have a microphone and an amplifier. They clipped the output of the amplifier to the wire terminals, and that drove the loudspeaker inside."

Bert clicked off his electric torch. "Eminently logical."

"Case closed?" Quack inquired.

"No," Ace said. "No, the violin is still quite as

deadly as ever, and I haven't a clue why."

CHAPTER 8

The next day, P. Charles Derkin sat at his dining room table and gushed, "I'm so glad I thought to hire you. A wind machine, of all things. A loudspeaker. How mundane! I feel like a man freed from prison."

The brighter Derkin's smile shone, the deeper Ace's scowl furrowed. She, Derkin, Quack, and Bert were just tucking away the last of the breakfast toast. Ace excused herself and prowled off like a restless panther. From the candlestick telephone in the living room, she asked the operator to connect her to the New York office.

"Carroway and Associates," droned a familiar voice.

"Mrs. Figgins. Ace, here. Did Sam or Gooper telegram?"

"Yes, ma'am. Mr. Biming did, from Danzig about two hours ago."

"Read it to me."

"Got your telegram, stop. E B jumped from window, stop. Impaled on wrought iron gate spikes, stop. Neighbor says suicide note fake, stop. Will inquire at police next, stop. S R B stop."

"E. B. is Ekaterina Brusikova, and S. R. B. is Sam Raia Biming," Ace murmured. "All right, thank you, Mrs. Figgins. There is no need to reply. It seems as if Sam is on the case."

"Very good, ma'am."

"Anything else urgent come up?" Ace asked.

"No, ma'am. Aeronautics called to say *Sky Arrow Two* passed the pressurization tests."

"Good."

"A Mr. Farnesworth of General Foods wants your picture for advertising breakfast cereal. Offered three thousand."[4]

"Tell him to go soak himself in milk."

"Already have done, ma'am."

"Thank you, Mrs. Figgins."

"My pleasure."

Ace stalked back into the dining room, where the men were enjoying tea. Her scars amplified her dour expression, and the sight of her stormy mien froze them mid-sip. She zeroed in on the violinist. "Mr. Derkin. I would like to insert a pulse transmitter into your violin case. It should slip in between the plush and the outside wall. You won't much notice the extra weight."

Derkin could hardly refuse. He fetched the violin from the heavy safe in his music parlor. Ace did swift surgery on the violin case, albeit with a sharp knife instead of a scalpel. She slipped a small bundle of wires and boxes underneath the padding.

Derkin held the Cremona Cannon nervously, plucking a pizzicato melody now and then. "What does it do?"

Bert tapped the side of his nose wisely. "If the violin is stolen, we can track it, that's all."

Ace reassembled the case. With its padding back in place, it looked unaltered. "I wired in an extra battery,

---

[4] About the price of a luxury car.

and I spaced the pulses to one ping per second. That, along with Tombstone's[5] efficient crystal oscillator, will conserve the battery life. It has limited range, though. Three miles, perhaps."

"You think this is necessary?" Derkin's brow wrinkled.

Ace slid the case back to him. "Hopefully not. Humor me."

Derkin chuckled warmly, a changed man from the quivering creature that had massacred his hat in the Carroway and Associates office. He bowed with a flourish. "Anything for you, Miss Carroway!"

"Fair enough," Ace said humorlessly. "Bert. Quack. We're taking off. Mr. Derkin, I'd appreciate it if you stayed near your phone today. If you don't mind, we'll be watching your house during the night."

Derkin's eyes grew rounder. "Oh! Well. All right."

Ace drove the purring roadster toward downtown Toronto, but her eyes focused beyond the parade of buildings. Quack, next to her in the passenger seat, said, "Penny for your thoughts."

Ace shot him a glance and a rueful smile. "I'm worried."

"About?"

"We tipped our hand before we knew a thing about

---

[5] Gregory "Tombstone" Jamison is the fifth of the five associates. He is an electrical and radio engineer. At the time of this story, he rode range in South Dakota, helping his sister build a fence.

whoever is stalking Derkin."

Quack and Bert exchanged glances. Quack stroked his beard. "We figured out the spook angle."

Bert said, "Did we? What was the purpose of haunting Derkin?"

"To scare him, I guess," Quack said.

"Sure." Bert's cane leaned between his knees. He tapped it against the floorboards for emphasis. "But why is a scared Derkin better than a calm Derkin?"

"Beats me," Quack said. "Although an individual under stress will often make poor decisions."

Ace zoomed around a slower car. "Let's review. P. Charles Derkin was left alone before he was given the Cremona Cannon. Now, he is being harassed. Ekaterina Brusikova, the previous owner, may or may not have been murdered. I hope Sam can find out more in Danzig. Thorpe G. Scott, the owner previous to that, also died in a bizarre way. Between owners, this ISPHA organization keeps the violin locked up. What do you make of all that?"

There was more mulling, then Bert guessed, "The violin really is cursed?"

Simultaneously, Quack said, "Greed?"

Ace turned two corners in rapid succession. "I don't know the answer. I was just seeing if you two had ideas. A curse is, of course, something I'd prefer to not believe in. It would throw my worldview into a tailspin. The notion of greed has some merit, but this violin is so famous, and its sound is so recognizable, that it could never be sold to a player. The first knowledgeable person to hear it played would know. I'm stymied."

Ace swerved once more, into a parking lot.

Bert's brow furrowed as he peered out the window. "So, we are going to the library?" Large letters on the building they approached spelled Toronto Reference Library.

"I am, at any rate. I want to get the list of all previous owners of the Cremona Cannon and research the International Society for the Protection of Historical Artifacts. You fellas can go get supplies for tonight's stakeout. Warmer clothing, for example. Maybe some dry snacks and a canteen of water."

After their supply run, Quack and Bert wandered the library stacks. Scents of old ink and paper permeated the hushed, hallowed halls. At a corner table, they discovered a semicircular pile of books. At its center, Ace's disheveled golden head pored over a thick biographical reference volume under the heading "Varque d'Rasque." Without looking up, she slid a sheet of paper across the table in the direction of her associates.

Bert and Quack glanced at each other, then at the sheet of paper. Quack picked up the sheet. Ace's foreshortened handwriting made a neat column down the left side of the page.

"List of owners of the Cremona Cannon," read Quack. He read slowly in an effort not to stumble over the names. "Pietr Vaskii, Varque d'Rasque, Glendon Snickett, ISPHA, and then the people we know: Scott, Brusikova, and Derkin."

Bert said, "Varque d'Rasque. That name does ring a

bell, but not about violins or music."

Quack continued to read, "ISPHA was created by an international treaty in the closing days of the Great War to preserve and protect stolen Ottoman treasures. Any recovered items of historical and artistic value were returned to their rightful owners if possible."

Bert's brow wrinkled. "Was the Cremona Cannon stolen by the Ottomans?"

Quack read, "Glendon Snickett smuggled the Cannon from Sögel, Germany, to Paris in the opening days of the Great War."

Bert chuckled. "I guess that's a yes."

Quack said, "Let me finish, you showboat. The last bits say that papers transferring ownership to Snickett were shown to authorities. The Cannon was kept in The Louvre for a short time. When Paris was threatened by Ottoman invasion, it was transferred to London."

Ace flipped a page in her book, reading avidly and at great speed. Her arm thrust out, and she tapped an archived newspaper, open on the tabletop.

Quack obediently started scanning the page. "*London Times*, dated the last year of the Great War. The headline is: Glendon Snickett missing, presumed dead. The article says: Famed explorer Glendon Snickett, climber of Mt. Kilimanjaro and rescuer of Ottoman art treasures, is reported lost behind enemy lines. Military sources say the Irishman went missing while trying to rescue French paintings from castle Schwarzerstein in Bavaria. The sources say that he is likely dead, although no attempt to recover his body is possible at this time. A more complete obituary will be published tomorrow."

Ace came to the end of her biography. She leaned back and laced her hands behind her head. Surveying the dapper gentlemen with eyes half-lidded, she said, "Just so. The name on the transfers was Varque d'Rasque. D'Rasque himself placed the Cremona Cannon in Glendon Snickett's hands and begged him to smuggle it out of the Ottoman Empire's reach."

Bert propped both hands on his cane. "And who was Varque d'Rasque? I swear I've heard that name before."

"He was an inventor. It's hard to get complete information about him because he was Ottoman or at least lived in Ottoman territory. It appears he progressed in rocketry, designed a better continuous tread for tanks, suggested changes for lightweight aircraft engines, and worked on the chemistry of explosives."

Bert adjusted his cuff links. "The inventor. That's right. I remember now."

Quack mused, "An Ottoman? Was he a violinist as well as an inventor?"

Ace's lips curled in a wry half-smile. "I can find no mention of it. He lived in Sögel all his days. His days ran out sometime during the Great War. So I have to assume he was not a musician."

Quack stroked his trim beard. "And yet he possessed a famous violin."

Bert slid his eyes to the scarred pilot. "Say, would Varque d'Rasque have worked for Darko Dor?"

"Yes, probably." Ace's mouth was a tight, thin line.

Quack said, "All right. Who was this first guy, Pietr Vaskii?"

Ace shook her head from side to side. "A collector, not a player. He was a rich industrialist. He owned mines and forests and steelworks, mostly in Prussia. Honestly, I stopped digging back in time once I found Varque d'Rasque. I have a hunch he's the key because of the incongruity."

"Ace, you're turning into Gooper," Quack said, "Incon-what-now?"

Ace flashed a brief grin. "I mean it's odd. He was a brilliant inventor who *just happened* to have a famous violin, even though he didn't play. At least, he didn't play professionally. As regards the case we're on, something must set the Cremona Cannon apart from other famous violins, and I'm betting it's somehow related to d'Rasque."

"It's a good hunch. How do we find out more?" Bert asked.

"Get me to a phone. I'll ask Mrs. Figgins to telegram Sam and Gooper."

There were public phones at the library. The operator rang up New York.

"Carroway and Associates."

"Mrs. Figgins. It's Ace again. Did Sam write back?"

"Yes, ma'am. Let me get the telegram. Got it. It says: Police say suicide note was typed but E K typewriter was not used, stop. Police think murder but have no suspects, stop."

A melodic trill diffused into being in the air. The warble was hard to locate. Its rise and fall caressed the ear, eerie yet beautiful. People in the library quested fruitlessly for the source. Quack and Bert grew smiles of anticipation. They knew the sound and its meaning. Ace had just made progress on the case. They nudged the pilot. "Well?"

Ace covered the mouthpiece for a moment. "Brusikova was murdered." She spoke to New York again. "Mrs. Figgins, please take this down. A telegram for Sam in Danzig. Ready?"

"Ready, ma'am."

"Please investigate Varque d'Rasque." Ace paused to spell that out for Mrs. Figgins. "Look for a connection to the Cremona Cannon violin in the region of Sögel, Germany. Send information to Mrs. Figgins. A life may depend on it."

"You just made Sam's day, Ace!" chuckled Quack.

"Thank you, Mrs. Figgins." Ace hung up. "What time is it?"

"About five o'clock," Bert replied.

"Right. Quick supper. Quick nap. Then to the stakeout."

GUY WORTHEY

CHAPTER 9

Sunset's rosy hues had faded to bruised purples among stretched-taffy clouds when they returned to P. Charles Derkin's house. Ace and her associates wore black coveralls, and Quack covered his blond hair with a stocking cap. As they crept into their now-traditional surveillance spruce, Bert pointed toward the house. "Look!"

Isabella Rosavino's little red Alpha Romero sat by the front porch. As they watched, the front door opened. In the yellow rectangle, the silhouette of the couple was plain. Isabella stood on tiptoe, her arms stretched around the neck of Charles. The watchers could almost taste the goodnight kiss. After the lingering, tender touch, Isabella slipped into her car and rolled away. The front door closed.

Bert exhaled, puffing out his cheeks. "Ace, I don't suppose you'd consider a night on the town with me some ti—"

Quack elbowed him in the ribs. "Down, boy!"

The darkness under the spruce rendered Ace's facial expression unreadable. "Never mix business with pleasure."

"Right. No pleasure." Bert huffed. "Meaning I can't pummel the smug off Quack's face, either."

Night spread across the city like a blanket of ink. Restless sighs of wind and a muted fizz of distant city traffic caressed the ear. The crescent moon approached first quarter. It shone intermittently between rapid clouds, but its dim light would not last long. Chasing the sun, its westward course would carry it below the horizon in a few hours.

Ace said, "I don't know what to expect, if anything. Let's move in closer. Quack, watch the front. I'll go around the side. Bert, 'round back. I'll hoot like an owl three times at the top of each hour. Hoot once if something happens. It could be a long night."

It was a chilly, lonely stakeout. The hours dragged by. Twice, triple owl hoots sounded, and then Derkin's bedroom light went dark. Another triple owl hoot sounded as the moon set. The clouds thinned, and the sky grew starry. Quack wished Bert were near, so he could gripe at him. Quack yawned and almost missed the quiet crunching of gravel from the driveway. He clapped his mouth shut and listened again, but the sound did not repeat.

Quack's eyes strained. He thought he saw black blobs moving by the front door. Was the front door opening? The blobs changed shape and then shrank and disappeared. There was a distinct click as the front door closed. Quack was suddenly wide awake, but he wasn't sure if he trusted his eyes.

The actor hooted. He was pleased at his performance, given the lack of rehearsal time.

Ten heartbeats later, a shadow materialized by his side. The formless shade whispered, "What's up?"

"Ace. I think some people went in the front door. They breezed in like it wasn't even locked!"

"Let's go see."

They crept to the front door. Quack laid a hand on the latch and carefully squeezed. The mechanism responded without complaint, and the bolt slid back.

Quack cracked the door open slowly. He felt Ace looking over his shoulder as they both strained to penetrate the gloom inside the widening vertical crack.

Seeing and hearing nothing, the two slipped inside, mincing on cat feet.

After only a few steps, rough voices growled from upstairs.

"Gotcha, fiddler!"

"Shaddap and head downstairs!"

Derkin's voice quavered faintly, "Wh-wh-what? Who are you?"

An electric light clicked on, illuminating the staircase and almost the whole ground floor.

Behind them, the front door slammed shut.

Ace and Quack pivoted toward the door, hearts in their throats. A thick figure stood wide-legged in the gloom. Goggles covered his eyes, and a grin plastered across his face. Much more impressively to Ace and Quack, his ham hand encased a large-bored pistol. The bruiser said in brusque tones, "Stay a while, why don'tcha? And don't try anything funny." The steadiness of the deadly revolver convinced Quack and Ace to hold still.

The thick man raised his gravelly voice. "Boss, we got company!"

A clear reply in British accents came from the stairs. "Where? Inside or out?" Ace and Quack swiveled their heads around to view the staircase. Derkin led the way, hands held awkwardly in front of his body, cuffed with metal rings. Two men followed, dressed in dark colors.

The door guard said with pride, "I got 'em here, inside." He stuck his gun in Quack's back. "Hold your hands high, where I can see 'em! Yeah, that's it.

Frankie, come frisk 'em."

"Frankie" separated from "Boss" and shuffled over to roughly pat down Quack. Skinnier and sweatier than the thug at the door, Frankie removed an electric torch from Quack's belt. Swatting rough hands against Ace, he sounded surprised in New Jersey accents. "Dis one's a dame."

The door guard snorted. "And mebbe money's green? Whatta genius you are, Frankie."

Ace growled like a hive full of half-awakened bees, and Frankie hastened his search. He plucked a second torch and also a screwdriver from her flight suit. Quack knew many more small items resided in small pockets sewn into the wide belt, but he wasn't about to start volunteering extra information.

"No guns or knives, boss," Frankie said.

All three intruders wore goggles over their eyes. The boss addressed Quack and Ace in a greasy north England accent, "That's good. Keep your head, and keep calm. You wouldn't want the musical bloke to get 'urt." He pointed an even larger pistol at Derkin's back and pushed him with it. "Get to the safe. Then open it. Anything goes wrong, I shoot you."

Quack noticed the thudding of his own heartbeat in his ears and the fact that the revolver held by the boss was oversized in every way. One could lose a quarter down the barrel bore.

Propelled by deadly steel at his back, a sweating, trembling Derkin lurched into his music studio. Quack and Ace exchanged an inconclusive glance and followed meekly. They all watched Derkin's normally dexterous fingers fumble at the safe's rotary dial.

Ace asked, as if commenting on the flavor of

teatime scones, "So, you've been playing ghost for a while. But now what? Plan B?"

Frankie snickered from behind them. "Yeah, the psychology tricks didn't pan out. Stupid violinist. He didn't follow any of the bait we dangled."

The boss stabbed a finger at the goon. "Shut it, Frankie! Amateur. Why don't you just hand over your birth certificate while you're blabbing? These are private detectives, you great git." While he was talking, Ace noticed a small gap between his top front teeth. The detail rattled around in her mind like a puzzle piece not yet ready to fall into place.

The boss turned his attention back to the kneeling Derkin. He jabbed him in the back with the overlarge revolver. "Come on! Get with it!"

"I … I'm trying! I think I messed it up," Derkin shakily replied. He spun the dial to clear it.

Quack glanced behind him. A sulkily frowning Frankie appeared unarmed, but the thick man with the gun still grinned at him, as if daring him to try something. The rangy actor faked a smile. "I guess there's no use getting hurt over a violin."

"You got that right, Cap!"

There was tense silence for a few more seconds. Quack listened to the throb of his own pulse and the precise clicks of the safe tumblers.

Finally, Derkin reached for the main latch and twisted it, then pulled. The heavy steel safe door opened.

The boss motioned with his gun and brayed, "Awright! Everybody, get by the piano! You, too, Derkin."

Derkin, Ace, and Quack made an awkward and reluctant trio by the piano.

The boss reached into the safe and snatched the sturdy violin case. He commanded the thick man and Frankie, "Guard my back. Make sure they don't follow." He snarled at Ace, Quack, and Derkin. "And you lot, don't follow. You look better without bullet holes. Just stay safe right there for half an hour."

The boss whirled and jogged out of sight through the music room doorway. Quack felt Ace tap on his elbow. The light touch signified action to come. Quack didn't move, except for a small upward tick at the corners of his lips.

When the thick man's eyes flicked to follow the boss, Ace pounced. She chopped brutally downward on the fellow's gun arm and followed that with a right uppercut to his jaw. The gun clattered to the floor, and the power of Ace's punch made the thug's skull resonate like a bongo drum.

Quack leapt at Frankie with less surgical precision but plenty of enthusiasm. He pounded his fists in a flurry at Frankie's face. Some of his blows penetrated Frankie's upraised forearms.

Derkin gulped and clutched at his heart. "Oh, my!"

The voice of the boss floated back from the front hall. "Bloody 'ell!"

The thick man wobbled with eyes gone glassy then collapsed in a limp heap of insensate limbs. Frankie, overwhelmed by Quack's onslaught, tried to scramble after the boss, but a boot from Ace downed him emphatically.

Three odd gun-like pops echoed from the front hall, like glass-coated firecrackers. The front door slammed.

Ace and Quack raced toward the front.

They did not get far. Hisses filled the living room, as if several enraged cobras had been let loose.

Quack's nose wrinkled, and his eyes started to water. Ace's arm swung like a bar across his chest, holding him back. She barked, "Xylyl bromide. Get Derkin out the back door before the gas gets to him."

"Tear gas!" Quack screeched, backpedaling frantically.

CHAPTER 10

He and Ace dashed back into the music studio. As a team, they latched onto Derkin and hustled him to the back door. The pain in Quack's eyes grew until tears streamed down his face. Finally, they fumbled their way through the extra locks and out into the dark night.

Once outside, Ace shouted, "Bert! If you can hear me, get to the front of the house and stop the man trying to get away!"

Quack muttered between gulps of fresh air, "That's what the big revolver was? A tear gas gun?"

"Horrid beasts!" Derkin said. "I'm shaking. Worst case of nerves I've ever had. Ouch. My eyes are watering."

Ace tugged at Derkin's and Quack's arms. "Come on, as fast as you can. We have to try to stop the thief."

None of them could sprint, not even Ace. Their eyes stung like forty sleepless nights. Besides the effects of the tear gas, the electric lights inside had blasted their night vision away. They bumbled through the inky night around the outside of the house. Unseen landscaping stones tripped them. Invisible shrubs clutched at them with twig fingers.

Ace arrived at the driveway first. She halted, senses straining. As Derkin and Quack arrived, she whirled toward the street, hands poised in a Wing Chun[6] defensive posture.

A manlike shape emerged from the darkness. His upraised hand blurred to a pale blob in the dark night. "No, Ace, don't punch. It's just me."

Quack whooshed a gust of breath. "Bert! There you are!"

Bert said, "Yes, yes, though I got clipped on the temple. I might be bleeding."

"The thief!" Quack said. "He got away."

"After I disarmed him, yeah. It was a short fight, but I was winning when he ran off. A clean escape."

"Rats!" Quack said.

"Bert? What's that in your hand?" Ace asked.

"What, this thing?" Bert drawled. "I'm no appraiser, but it's got all the earmarks of being the Cremona Cannon."

"What?" Quack blurted.

"I win the prize this time, you hapless hack. Here, Ace," Bert said. "My electric torch. Shine a light on it, just to be sure."

Ace beamed the light toward the end of the driveway first, but there was no one and nothing to be seen. After a frustrated huff, she played the light on the violin case held by Bert.

Derkin said, "That's it, all right."

Quack said gently, "You don't sound one hundred percent happy about that, friend."

"I'm not." Derkin spat. "The violin's cursed! Just not in the way I was thinking before."

---

[6] From a young age, Ace received training in the martial art of Wing Chun by Master Jitsuko of Osaka.

♠ ♠ ♠

The night was far from over. The police were summoned. Slowed by the lingering toxic gas, they eventually extracted the unconscious thieves. After they gave their statements to the police, the four protectors of the Cremona Cannon opened all the windows to let the house air out. They quit the premises and drove.

"Charles," Ace said from the driver's seat, "one of the crooks scolded you for not following 'bait.' Who can you think of that has been asking for the violin? Or, perhaps, asking for you?"

"Eh? Well, I got a telegram about a memorial concert for Ekaterina Brusikova, inviting me to play," the violinist replied from the back seat. His hands twitched atop the violin case that rested on his lap.

"Where? When?"

"Three weeks from now, in Danzig. It's short notice, but I would like to go if I could manage it. Brusikova was a giant. She could make audiences cry or dance, according to her musical interpretation of the moment. It would be an honor to pay her some homage."

"Interesting. Any other requests of you? Any strangers contacting you?"

"I can't think of—" The violinist blinked. "Wait. There was a repair shop. Blake Violins. They wanted to adjust my sound post free of charge. I told them no, of course. I'm not going to let some shop I've never heard of handle my violin."

"Hm. That could be it. What about Isabella Rosavino?"

Derkin said mildly, "No, we still couldn't arrange those photographs."

Ace pursed her lips. "She asked?"

"She mentioned it," Derkin said. "She doesn't seem to be in a hurry to get it done."

"She likes you," Bert said.

Derkin's face flushed, and his lips tightened.

Ace pressed, "Did she have a business card? Or mention her employer?"

The violinist's eyebrows worked. "I have an impression she did. Now that you ask in such a way, though, I'm not sure."

"All right, fair enough." Ace drummed her thumbs on the steering wheel. "Let's hope the thieves we caught talk after they wake up."

She pointed forward. "Look, a hotel. The Open Arms. I've never heard of it."

"Perfect for laying low in," said Bert.

"Just so."

Coming up next evening, Derkin had a rehearsal with the symphony. During the day, Ace and her associates let him attend to his business while they engaged in old-fashioned gumshoeing. They visited the police station and the hospital, finding out the status of Frankie and his thicker companion. Both henchmen lay in beds with their mouths and noses covered by masks hooked to oxygen tanks. The tear gas had burned their lungs, and it would be some time before they could talk. The Toronto police had not yet identified them.

Ace and associates searched for Blake Violins but did not find it. They even inquired at Derkin's favorite shop, but the craftsmen said they had never heard of it. They gave up and drove back to the rehearsal hall.

"No such place as Blake Violins. So, what was that about? They were hoping to get the Cremona Cannon by posing as a fake violin shop?" Bert pondered.

"That's my take," Quack agreed.

"Say." Bert shot a glance at Ace. "Is Miss Rosavino a suspect?"

"Of course," Ace said. "She showed up after the violin."

"Oh, no! With all the romancing going on? I don't believe it." Quack frowned.

"Well, it's one possible way to separate the violin and Derkin. It's just not as overt as the thuggery of last night." Ace parked her roadster by an antique theater, the site of Derkin's symphony rehearsal.

They piled out of the spotless machine. Bert scanned the façade of the hall. "Lovely place to rehearse, I'd say." But the front door did not budge.

"Oh, it's not concert night yet," Quack said. "Stage entrance, then. It'll be around back."

They sauntered around the block to the rear of the building. A delivery truck squatted there with its back doors wide open. As the associates reached for the latch on the stage entrance, it popped open and a pair of workmen lumbered out, wheeling a large papier-mâché tree trunk.

"'Scuse us, ma'am! Aboot ran into you there!" the one with the big black mustache said with a quick grin at Ace.

Bert snorted. "Stage props. This place is right up your alley, Quack."

The doorway soon cleared, and the trio walked in. They could hear the soft magic of a rehearsing symphony as soon as they entered the cluttered backstage area.

Ace's footsteps slowed. Her eyebrows knitted.

Bert and Quack got a few paces ahead, then turned around to view Ace and her scrunched-up forehead.

"What's wrong, Ace?" Bert asked.

Ace's golden eyes were unfocused. She appeared to be thinking furiously.

From deeper inside the building floated an accented female voice. "Ah, signori, I am glad to see your handsome faces!"

Quack and Bert pivoted to see Isabella Rosavino approach. Moony smiles stole over their faces.

"Got it!" Ace interrupted with crisp urgency. Her associates whipped their heads back around. "He had a gap between his front teeth. Come on!"

"What?" Quack blurted.

"Huh?" Bert said.

But Ace pelted back the way they had come.

Pulses suddenly pounding, Quack and Bert leapt to pursue like runners coming off their starting blocks. Isabella chased them, calling, "Come back! Charles Derkin, he is not here. I cannot find him."

They burst back out through the stage doors into the back alley. The delivery truck roared away, accelerating to a reckless speed.

Ace put her head down and sprinted. Her swift calculations worked out in her favor. Surely she could hitch a ride on the rear bumper before the truck entered traffic.

Bert and Quack pounded along behind and saw Ace dash forward like a streak. Quack caught a glimpse of a man leaning out of the passenger seat of the truck. In his hands, the lumpy outline of a Thompson machine gun showed.

"Look out!" Quack bellowed.

The tommy gun spoke in a deadly staccato. Bullets ricocheted down the alley. The line of spraying bullets zeroed in on Ace.

CHAPTER 11

Ace veered left. She avoided the deadly line of flying lead, but her violent course change sent her into a cluster of trash barrels. Flesh and metal collided. The barrels fairly exploded in a cacophony of metallic banging. Ace's prone body rolled over and over before flopping to a stop.

The truck escaped into the street.

Bert and Quack pounded up. "Ace! Ace, are you all right?"

Ace groaned. Quack and Bert hovered, faces dismayed. Ace peered at them woozily. "Help me up, fellas." A cut above her unscarred temple oozed sluggish red.

Between them, they raised Ace to unsteady feet.

"Are you really all right?" Quack's brow furrowed.

"I'll be fine. That sure rang my bells, though." She grimaced. "We need to make chainmail underwear or something. Have you noticed that we tend to get shot at a fair amount?"

"You're okay!" Bert blew air into his cheeks, relieved. The two flanked Ace, supporting her.

Isabella Rosavino caught up, elegant heels clacking on the pavement. "Miss Carroway, you are somehow unhurt? But Mr. Derkin! He is gone! What is going on? Were those Chicago gangsters?"

"Derkin is gone?" Quack blurted.

71

Ace said grimly, "He's in that truck, I bet. The workman that said hello to me had a gap between his front teeth. So did the ringleader from last night. And, come to think of it, so did the custodian at the New York concert when Derkin's violin popped its tailgut."

"The same guy?" Quack slapped his own forehead. "I should have spotted that."

"Charles is kidnapped?" Isabella was aghast.

"And the violin, too, probably," Bert said softly.

"Oh, no! What shall we do?" Isabella said.

"Let go of me. I can walk," Ace said, tearing free of Quack and Bert. She lurched along through the alley, following the truck. Cautious, silent passersby had appeared at the intersection, wide-eyed and nervous after the gunfire in their neighborhood.

"There must be a telephone in the theater." Isabella gestured wildly, pointing back toward the hall where the symphony rehearsed. Inside, sixty musicians played on, unaware of the drama unfolding just outside their pocket of peace and beauty.

Ace approached the nearest citizen, a white-haired man in a rumpled suit. "You saw the white truck?"

He nodded.

She said, "Call the police. Tell them it's a kidnapping."

"Yes, ma'am," said the fellow. With a tip of his hat, he strode away.

"A kidnapping!" the onlookers echoed.

Ace's limp lessened as she moved on around the corner. She said over her shoulder, "Come on!"

The shapely photographer hovered near, forehead scrunched up, hands wringing together. Bert beamed her a gallant smile. "Miss Rosavino, with all that shooting, I'm sure the police are already on their way. You should go back to the theater."

"No, no, no. I am coming with you. You are the detectives he hired to keep him *safe*, yes?" Isabella's dark eyes flashed in accusation.

Bert, Quack, and Isabella jogged to catch up to Ace, whose limp had all but disappeared. Around the block they raced, and darted into the four-door roadster. Ace did not comment as Isa slipped into the back seat.

Quack, in the passenger seat, extracted a metal loop and earphones from the modified glove compartment. He plugged them both into a rack with a row of knobs and meters.

"That," Bert explained to his back seat companion, Isabella Rosavino, "is a loop antenna. It allows us to track the stolen violin."

"What?" Isabella's groomed eyebrows worked. "How is that possible?"

Bert said, "Erm. I'm just a lawyer. It goes beep beep beep. Quack rotates the loop until the beeps are the loudest, and that's the direction to go."

Quack said, "Signal's strong. Turn left at the next main road."

"That is amazing," Isabella said.

Ace drove faster than the Toronto traffic, using the roadster's engine to power around slower cars. Generally, the radio pulses steered them eastward. She glanced into the rearview mirror. "Miss Rosavino, we may be shot at. There is considerable danger. If you choose to stay, I cannot be responsible for your safety."

"I stay!" Isabella said, stamping her foot.

Bert looked at her with admiration. She glanced

outside. Bert followed her gaze.

"Ace!" he blurted. "The truck! Down the side street we just passed!"

Ace veered onto the next cross street and caused a danger-conscious Toronto driver to honk. She headed on around the block. Quack said, "The tracker says: not this way. The pulse is still east of us."

The roadster screeched to a halt beside the white delivery truck. Quiet apartments lined the tree-shaded street. Everyone piled out, moving with exaggerated caution. They peered in the front windows. Empty. They cautiously skirted to the truck's rear. Ace and Quack gripped the rear door handles. At a nod, they both ripped open the unlocked doors, ready to dodge gunfire.

But the truck was unoccupied. By people, that is. The truck was about half full of the papier-mâché tree trunk prop. Quack poked at it. It was lightweight and hollow.

Bert said, "They switched vehicles?"

Ace's eyes roved the interior. "Evidently."

Quack groaned. "I bet whatever they're driving now is race car fast!"

Ace murmured, "Faintly, I smell chloroform."

"Will we chase them more?" Isabella wondered.

"Do lawyers lie?" Quack answered.

As they swarmed back into the C. Carroway & Associates company roadster, Bert the lawyer grit his teeth. "Hack!"

Quack waggled blond eyebrows at him.

CHAPTER 12

With metallic determination in her steady eyes, Ace drove faster and faster, weaving her way through traffic. Quack reported on the strength and direction of the pulses. Steadily, they gained ground. With a squeal of rubber, they veered onto the highway to Montreal. Traffic thinned. Dusk fell. Ace finally unleashed the full power of the roadster's engine, and they all but flew down the highway.

They zipped past an Alvis Firebird with children in the back seat and caught sight of a car ahead of them, moving fast.

Ace squinted. "A Cadillac Sixteen. Looks new. How's the signal, Quack?"

"Loudest yet, Ace!"

"All right. Ladies and gentlemen, whatever we do is going to be risky. I propose we drive alongside and pop their tire. There's a Colt in the—"

"Got it already, Ace!" Quack grinned, waving a six-shooter in the air.

"Brilliant." Ace pressed the accelerator flat to the floor. Quack rolled his window down, and a roar of buffeting wind filled the interior. Ace switched lanes.

A tommy gun had emerged from the Cadillac's left rear window. It was followed by a shoulder and head. The muzzle began flashing.

"Duck!" Bert screeched.

The hail of bullets spattered on the windshield, making a row of holes surrounded by spiderweb patterns of cracks.

Ace slammed a foot on the brake pedal.

Everybody lurched forward. The gunfire stopped. Ace matched speed again, but at a generous distance behind, too far for anything but the luckiest bullet to hit them. Solemnly, Quack rolled the window back up.

"So," Bert observed as he untangled himself from Isabella. "They got a machine gun."

Quack cleared his throat. "And they're awfully eager to use it."

Isa lifted her head from Bert's lap and sat upright. "I worry. Was I too hasty when I demand to come?" The photographer gripped the seat cushion with fingers tense as claws.

Ace said, "Perhaps we can race past them and—Oh, no!"

Ahead of them, muzzle fire flashed, aimed toward an oncoming heavy truck. Tires blew out in an explosion of rubber bits. Sparks flew as the bare rims dipped to touch the asphalt. The truck veered, ponderously spinning broadside and spanning both lanes of the highway.

Collision seemed both imminent and inevitable.

Ace's mouth compressed to a hard line. She spun the steering wheel hard left. The rubber of the roadster's wheels screamed and smoked. The change of direction pinned her passengers to the right side of the car's body.

The truck tipped and slid on its side, erupting showers of sparks brilliant in the dim dusk. It covered both lanes of the road and more, a gigantic rectangular piston. The roadster dove off the pavement and sailed airborne over the ditch. It missed the hurtling truck by inches and broke through a curtain of sparks.

"Hold tight!" advised Ace.

The roadster hit the far side of the roadside ditch with a bone-jarring wallop.

"Aiee!" Isabella cried.

The jostling improved little as Ace steered the car in a long arc through bumpy farmland.

"One more bump!" warned Ace, just before they leapt the ditch again. The car slid up the embankment to the paved road, and Ace braked to a stop.

She shifted to neutral and revved the willing engine. "Everybody in one piece?"

"Think so," Bert said, seeing stars.

Ace glanced at the receding dot of the Cadillac, then back toward the wrecked truck. She put the roadster in gear and peeled out.

But not back to the chase. Flames shot from the truck's underside, and Ace steered back toward the wreck.

"I definitely rethink now," Isabella said shakily.

"Um." Quack rubbed the corner of his eye. "We want to get *nearer* to the burning truck?"

Ace said grimly, "I think the driver's still in the cab. We have to get them out."

The undercarriage of the truck faced them as it lay on its side. Burning gasoline trailed away over the asphalt. Some of the tires were beginning to catch on fire. Acrid petroleum smoke choked the air. Ace bumped the nose of the roadster against the cab of the truck, as far from the flames as possible but still uncomfortably close.

"The roadster hood will boost us up there. Bert and Quack, help?"

The roadster erupted people. Isabella wobbled off to one side while Ace, Bert, and Quack swarmed up to the hood and thence up the truck cab. They wrestled the truck door open and peered down into the cab. The driver grimaced at them. He cradled a broken arm and seemed half dazed by the pain.

Ace dropped down into the sideways cab next to the sprawled driver. Using his water thermos, she bashed out the remainder of the broken windshield.

Isabella remembered the camera around her neck and snapped a picture of the fiery scene. "*Accidenti!* My flash bulb, she is broke!"

Bert and Quack dropped back to the pavement and raced to help Ace extract the injured man. Working as a team, the three of them slid the driver free. Burdened with his body, they shuffled well away from the growing fire and laid him out on the ground. By this time, several vehicles had collected at the crash scene.

"Get the first aid kit from the trunk of the roadster, Bert," Ace said over her shoulder. She met the driver's eyes with a sober gaze. "I need to straighten your arm and get a splint on it. I'll be as gentle as I can."

"All right," whispered the driver. His eyes rolled up in his head as the last shreds of consciousness left him.

Bert ran to the roadster, but it emitted a loud bang as he arrived. One of the tires had softened from the radiant heat of the burning truck and popped. The paint on the right side was blistering as well. He leapt behind the wheel and backed the roadster out of danger, but a second tire popped as he did.

Bert fetched the first aid kit as quickly as he could

and sprinted back to the injured man. As Ace held the driver's arm in traction, Quack splinted it in place. Isabella watched from a safe vantage, dark eyes big.

By the time fire trucks arrived, motorists had helped to quell the flames. The crisis ebbed.

"We can't chase the Cadillac anymore," Bert morosely observed. "Two tires popped, but we only have one spare."

Ace allowed her aching body to relax and plopped next to the prone truck driver. She let her head loll back to watch the timeless stars. "So be it. When we get to a phone, I have about ten percent of a new plan."

Quack nodded soberly. "Ten percent? Better than average."

CHAPTER 13

After hours of dealing with firefighters, police, by-standers, and tow truck drivers, the party lodged at the nearest roadside inn. They rented the only two remaining rooms. The men took one and the women the other.

After a bath, Isabella brushed her teeth. As she peeled her bedcovers down, Ace arrived.

"Your telephone calls, they went well?" Isabella asked.

"Yes, thank you. How are you doing, Isabella?" Ace locked the door behind her and leaned against it wearily.

"I am thinking I do better than you, Miss Carroway. I have only a few bruises, compared to your many. Can I call you Ace, like the men do?"

The corners of Ace's eyes crinkled. "Of course."

"I will try it, Ace. Ace. Ace. Si, si, I can do it." She winked. "Call me Isa."

"All right, Isa."

"Does it mean that you are a pilot? You dress like one."

"Yes, that's right. I love to fly." Ace unbuckled the belt of her flight suit.

"I see. Bella." Isabella gazed steadily at the flyer. "Ace, I have asked a favor of the older woman in the next room, and she has given us this." Isabella retrieved a mostly empty paper bag from the nightstand

and offered it to Ace.

"What? Oh! Is it Epsom salts?" Ace's golden eyes widened.

"Yes, Ace. Your bath will feel decadent, like a bath in Rome." Isabella's expressive lips curled in a wry tease of a smile.

"Thank you! I'm in your debt, Isa. This is just what the doctor ordered!" Ace cradled the bag of bath crystals reverently in two hands and carried it like a talisman into the bathroom.

Isabella chuckled. "I was thinking of myself, too, yes? But now I will wonder how you will repay this debt of which you speak." The photographer slipped under the covers and dozed.

Soft brushing sounds brought her awake again. The light in the bathroom was still on, dimly illuminating the hotel room. Isabella half sat up to discover the source of the noises. Ace was standing on her head on the floor, scissoring her legs slowly. The brush of fabric and Ace's regular, deep breathing sighed together like metronomes.

As Isabella watched, even Ace's head left the floor, her whole weight supported on fingertips alone. Ace's toes touched down near the back of her head, her back arching like an acrobat. Moving her center of gravity slightly, Ace unbent, this time supported by her feet. She came upright, arms spread wide like a swan.

Ace's and Isabella's eyes met.

Ace grimaced apologetically. "Sorry. Exercises. I wasn't quiet enough."

"No, no, no! I would not have missed it for the world. You are like a dancer. Or a circus person. But more than either of those."

Ace folded her legs to sit on the floor in a pose of meditation. "Thank you. Um. You can go back to sleep. I won't get any louder."

Isabella laughed. Even in the near darkness, her eyes sparkled. "You are shy? Do not be shy, Ace. I am learning about you. You are not a detective only. You have, ah, how was it said? Loop antennae. Yes, you have those, and handsome men, and fast cars, and now these exercises. And interesting underwear."

Isabella's foundation garment had spaghetti shoulder straps and clips for hosiery, but Ace's was either a plain swimsuit or a man's union suit.

Ace spluttered, "I ... well, I ..."

Isabella laughed even more richly. "You *are* shy! I am filled with delight. Ace, may I say? You are tall and fierce, with scars by one eye. I am wishing to know more things about you. I am too curious, I know. Some things I can understand. You are practical. You *must* wear a swimsuit for underwear, to exercise like you do. Anything else would rip and tear."

"I tend to be practical. It's one of my worst faults," Ace said, subdued. She watched Isabella's dark eyes dance.

"As you must. You beat all the men at their own game, yes? Oh, yes. Yes, I begin to see how it is with you, Ace. I am amazed."

"I, um," Ace stewed.

"Hush, now! Continue! I will be quiet. I will give you peace. But I will watch you finish, too. I cannot look away." Isabella fluffed a pillow behind her back and smiled like a mischievous imp.

Ace's lips twitched upwards uncertainly and she returned to her exercises. Begun in childhood, her daily routine strengthened her body, sharpened her senses, and expanded her mental powers. As grueling as the physical contortions appeared, her simultaneous mental gymnastics were twice as torturous. She solved logic puzzles, computed ancient dates, and pushed through the twists of advanced algebras.

Finally, Ace slipped under the covers for sleep. Despite bruises, fatigued muscles, and a tired brain, slumber did not immediately come. Did dark eyes observe her from the next bed? Did an inscrutable curve of lips send messages whose deeper meaning lay beyond Ace's grasp? Was Isa the flirtatious photographer she appeared to be, or was she playing a part? Could she know the secret of the deadly violin?

For Ace, the unsolved questions spun in her mind until they wove together into a cottony mass of doubt-filled dreams.

In the morning, Ace roused Isabella with a bright, "Rise and shine. Two eternities, the past and the future, meet in the here and now!"

Isabella buried her head under a pillow. "No. I am Italian. Do not wake me before noon."

"There might be coffee," Ace wheedled.

Isabella protested, "Lies. Dirty lies to trick me." But she peeked out from under the pillow.

After dressing, she wandered down to the tiny hotel's lobby. But Ace, Bert, and Quack stood outside the hotel's doors, staring south. When she joined them and followed their gaze, her sleepy eyes widened.

A stately dirigible glided on the morning air. The vast airship grew larger and larger, rosily lit from the east by the rising sun. Lettering on its side read "*Sky Arrow One.*" A minute later, Isabella realized that it was descending, heading for them.

"You? You summoned this?" she asked incredulously.

A smug aspect settled on Bert's face. "Working conditions will improve now."

"That's the prototype of Ace's production model dirigibles," Quack said.

"I'm a lucky woman," Ace said, gazing at *Sky Arrow One*, golden eyes gone dreamy. "But don't say it's mine. It belongs to the company."

Bert guffawed. "The company called Carroway Aeronautics, you mean?"

"What?" Isabella blurted. "I thought you were detectives!"

Quack said, with dignity, "We are. We're *well-equipped* detectives, that's all."

The dirigible hovered over their heads and pivoted its tail downwind with unhurried rotation. Ace said, "It would have been here sooner, but I asked for some specialty items to be stowed on board. Ah, here we go."

The airship touched down on a triangle of wheels, a gentle giant of the airways kissing the earth in a tease of neutral buoyancy. At the slightest provocation, it would bounce away, untouchable.

A ladder popped out of the back of the gondola, and two youths in white flight suits descended it nimbly, then flanked it like medieval guards. They kept a grip on the ladder with one hand, just in case a vagrant zephyr lifted the airship.

"Vivian! Gilbert! I'm glad to see you two!" Ace jogged over, grinning.

The two clean-cut teens said in unison, "At your service, Captain!"

"Ha!" chortled Ace. "You must've rehearsed that 'at your service' shtick. How's the *Sky Arrow*?"

"Raring to go," Gilbert said.

"All the way to Egypt, if necessary," Vivian added.[7]

A plump man descended the ladder, much more slowly than had Vivian and Gilbert. He exhaled in relief as he reached firm ground. He weakly smiled up at Ace. "Hullo, boss!"

"Bosley? From accounting?"

"Yes, for now." He puffed up his chest under his pinstriped suit. "I'm working my way up to associate."[8]

"Are you, now? I'll be sure to let you know if there's an opening." Ace thrust car keys at him. "The roadster's at Belleville Body and Towing. They promised it would be done before noon."

The accountant took the keys. "Oh. Yes, ma'am." He pivoted toward the hotel lobby, only to be brick walled by the sight of Isabella Rosavino. "M-m-ma'am!" he stammered.

On cue, Bert and Quack flanked Isabella and stuck

---

[7] Twins Vivian and Gilbert Fernwood were the crew of *Sky Arrow One*, whose maiden voyage took her from Lark Haven, Pennsylvania, to Meroë-inet in southern Egypt, as recounted in *Ace Carroway and the Midnight Scream*.

[8] Ace's five associates are Bert, Quack, Sam, Tombstone, and Gooper.

out their elbows. After a flirtatious glance left and right, she slipped her hands into the crooks of her escorts' arms and allowed them to guide her toward the airship. She winked at Bosley as she passed, but mostly her gaze riveted to the luminous airship.

Bert cast his own appraising eye upon the woman at his arm, then smirked at the stunned accountant. "Good luck making associate, Bosley. It's a wicked good gig, if I do say so myself."

Bosley's round eyes tracked Isabella as Bert and Quack handed her up into the gondola. He barely noticed the others going up and in. When the airship lifted off into the morning air, he watched it recede.

Finally, he pinched himself. He went to find some coffee.

Isabella found coffee, too, and a very comfortable lounge with a spectacular view. *Sky Arrow One* headed straight down the St. Lawrence, soon passing Montreal. Vivian attended the helm, while Gilbert saw to the comfort of the passengers.

"What a nice boy," Isabella said of Gilbert.

"I'm nice, too!" Bert assured her.

"Ugh." Quack glowered at Bert. He turned to Ace. "What was the morning phone call about?"

Ace replied, "Police in Montreal found the Cadillac Sixteen."

"That's good!"

"It's progress." Ace's face, however, remained sober. "The empty Cadillac sat by a vacant slip where a yacht called the *Tern* had been moored. It's a fast yacht with Turkish registry."

Isa sipped her coffee. "Charles is on this ship?"

"It stands to reason that he is, and the Cremona Cannon, too. The bad news is that there are no locks and dams between Montreal and the open ocean." She pursed her lips. "And the St. Lawrence is wide."

Bert said, "The police can't just stop the ship?"

Ace's eyes flicked forward to gaze through the gondola window at the aerial vista. "They cannot. Apparently, the police only have a few motorboats. They are not equipped to chase a fast yacht."

The dark-haired lawyer pursed his lips. "It's like they're pirates or something."

Quack glanced to Isabella and shifted his weight from foot to foot. Finally, he cleared his throat. "I hate to bring this up, but do you think P. Charles Derkin is truly aboard that ship? Or did they just dump him somewhere along the road?"

"Americans. So blunt!" Isabella lifted her chin. "But I am strong. I can face the truth."

Quack and Bert gazed at Isabella with a mix of admiration and sympathy.

Ace said, "I think the odds are in favor of kidnapping as opposed to some kind of gang-style murder. The conspiracy, whatever it is, could have come guns ablaze at any time, but they held off."

"Until they shot at you." Quack lifted an eyebrow.

Ace shot an amused glance at him. "Just so. By the way, we guessed correctly yesterday. The police confirmed that both Derkin and the Cremona Cannon were taken from the rehearsal hall. You'll recall the theater prop tree trunk? That was pre-planned to hide an unconscious body."

Isa clucked her tongue. "Terrible."

"How are we going to find that ship, Ace?" Bert asked. "The Atlantic Ocean's a big place, and the ping transmitter only ranges a few miles."

"We're going to need luck, but it won't be as bad as a whole ocean. We can catch them before they are out of the St. Lawrence mouth. At least, that's my hope. The loop receiver is already warm."

The airship cruised down the St. Lawrence until the lazy mouth of the giant river opened up to meet the Atlantic Ocean. When the river widened, the airship zig-zagged north and south while still heading generally eastward. A haze hung in the air that limited visibility. Gradually, the haze thickened.

No signal reached the loop receiver at which Ace listened with headphone speakers.

Eventually, Ace huffed air through her nose and frowned. With a finger, she tapped a map tacked up in the navigator's cubby. "They are ahead of us, going full steam, no doubt. Must be a fast ship. Now, here's where luck comes in. We have to guess if they are going to pass Labrador on the south or north. The strait to the north is much narrower. If they go that way, we will catch them if we lie in wait. The southern strait is at least fifty miles across. They could slip right by us." Ace pulled on her lower lip.

"They've been as unpredictable as a bribed witness so far," said Bert. "I bet they will continue to be a pain in the neck and go south."

South they went.

In the south strait they searched, but in vain. The

haze thickened. The sun crossed the sky and dropped into the west. Ace slumped lower and lower in the seat by the radio console. She had patched the mournful empty static from the loop antenna through a speaker so that everyone could hear.

Quack finally said softly, "We guessed wrong?"

Ace's shoulders fell another notch.

Bert answered in Ace's stead, "That's an affirmative, Quack. We gave up a sure thing to chase a great big nothing."

Ace straightened and grew a lopsided smile. "One more chance. The longest shot of all. Gilbert! New heading: thirty-five. North by northeast we sail. Into the gloom we pierce like an arrow of the sky. We'll try to find them by blind luck in the open sea."

"Charles. Oh, Charles," Isabella murmured around a knuckle held to her lips.

None found any words to comfort her.

The vigil continued. The engines droned. Vivian replaced Gilbert at the helm, and Gilbert headed aft to nap. The hours ticked by like glaciers grinding down a mountain.

Rubbing sleep out of her eyes, Ace gave the loop a dismissive spin. "All right. Enough's enough. We lost."

Insultingly, at long last, the speaker pinged a brief tone.

Ace reacted instantly, slapping her right hand on the rotary mount to stop the loop from spinning further. "Vivian! New heading! Eighty-five!"

"What? A pulse?" Quack groggily murmured.

"Uh-huh!" Ace gushed, then squinted. "But not a second one? Or was that it, very faint?"

Ace plugged headphones back in and frowned. She

nabbed a stub of a pencil and began taking notes. This went on for a long time. Once, she barked, "Vivian. Three degrees north," then returned to listening.

Bert and Quack found the new trace exciting for a while. But as time passed, Bert's face gradually fell. He murmured to Quack, "What's the range on the pulse transmitter again?"

"Three miles."

"And how long does it take the *Sky Arrow* to travel three miles?"

"Uhhhh, two or three minutes."

They looked at each other.

They looked at the clock. It had been more like ten.

Ace frowned and tapped her pencil stub on the paper. "Lost it entirely now! It was fading in and out. Sinusoidal pattern. It shouldn't do that!"

Bert and Quack exchanged mournful glances. Quack reached to place a hand on Ace's shoulder, but he snatched it back when she blurted, "It's back! Faint, but it's back."

A minute later, she reported, "Steady. Getting stronger. Vivian, throttle down to ten percent."

Ace nodded to Bert and Quack. "We found the pulse transmitter. Odds are decent we found everything. The *Tern*, P. Charles Derkin, and the Cremona Cannon, too."

Bert grinned like a wolf. "And some kidnapper heads to crack."

"True enough," Ace said, clearly distracted. She rested two fingers on her temple in thought. "What's bothering me is the behavior of the pulse transmitter. First, it was choppy but much, much longer range. Then, when we closed on its position, it behaved as I expected. What was boosting it?"

"Good luck?" Quack said with a dimpled smile.

"Ugh, Quack." Bert rolled his eyes.

Ace said, "There must be a reason. Physics demands it."

"Parabolic reflectors beam radio signals in one direction," said a voice. Every eye roved to discover who had spoken. It was Vivian. The teen helped herself to a sip of coffee.

An eerie, melodic warbling began to fill the cabin, beautiful and low. Although the sound seemed to have no source, caressing the ear from all directions equally, Bert and Quack snapped their heads around to stare at Ace. "What? You figured out something!"

But an enigmatic curve of Ace's lips was all the answer they received.

CHAPTER 14

The tracking pulses held steady, but squalls delayed action by two days and a night. Gusts tossed *Sky Arrow One* in slow, heaving motions reminiscent of travel by ocean liner. By the second night, the *Tern* had crossed more than half the Atlantic. It was evidently a speedy yacht, indeed. The upside of the foul weather was that the *Sky Arrow One* stayed hidden in the clouds, shadowing the yacht below like the ghost of a hunting eagle.

Airship life was spartan but comfortable in the gleaming gondola. Private cabins lay aft, an open lounge occupied the middle, and the controls clustered up front. Changes of clothing could be had aboard, but to Isabella's dismay, the only style available came in the form of a flight suit. She griped over breakfast, "In this, I look like a man."

Quack's eyebrows raised. "Let me assure you, Miss Rosavino, that is far from the case."

Bert nodded vigorously. "*Far* from the case."

"Oh, such charmers," she said. "Not to mention decorative, too."

The men sat straighter.

"I could maybe take in the waist for you," Ace volunteered, "while we wait for good weather."

"You could?" Isabella pinched the baggy canvas on her sides.

"Sure," Ace said. "Not like a tailor could, but

enough to show your thisses and thats."

Isa smoothed the fabric over her belly. "I'd like that."

Bert's lips shifted to one side. "See, if I had cracked a remark about Isa's thisses and thats, I'd probably get slapped."

The photographer's eyelids descended to cover half her eyes. "Miss Carroway has permission to discuss my figure."

Quack said aside to Bert, "I can slap you if you like."

Bert sneered. "You just try it."

"I just might." Quack stroked his chin. "It might lead to the job opening Bosley dreamt of."

Bert opened his mouth to reply, but Ace shuddered and raised a finger to interrupt. "No! Gadzooks, no. You fellas are it, so don't go killing each other."

Ace's horrified expression melted into a wide grin.

They all chuckled.

Finally, on the second night, with winds dying and stars twinkling through rips in the scudding clouds, Ace gave the go-ahead. A well-rehearsed but untried plan clicked into motion.

Running only one engine, the airship dropped so low that spindrift blown from the wave tops speckled the gondola windows. From behind the *Tern*, the starlit behemoth approached. As it slid over the deck, three ropes dropped and dangled from the gondola. Three dark shapes slipped down like beads on wires to the deck.

Like a gargantuan ghost, *Sky Arrow One* glided back into the sky as the trio of raiders scurried to find hiding places on the deck. The labored chugging of the

Tern's full tilt engines overwhelmed the drone of the silver dirigible's motor. The three hunkered down and exchanged glances, senses alert.

But no alarm rang out. Nobody shouted. Not a soul was visible on deck. Ace motioned forward.

Bert and Quack darted toward ventilation intakes. They unslung their packs and slid large metal canisters out. Exchanging grins, they placed several bottles of compressed gases into the air intakes, then opened the stopcocks. A bubbling sound commenced, and Bert and Quack plopped gas masks on over their faces. The contraptions covered nose and mouth, hooked by a tube to an air tank on their backs.

Meanwhile, Ace padded to the wheelhouse on cat feet. She found the helmsman half dozing at the wheel, staring forward, unaware of the airship or the invaders.

Ace flung the door open. The helmsman pivoted and his eyes widened, and those actions were all he could manage before Ace's hand closed upon his neck. With precise placement and pressure, fingers more like iron than flesh squeezed off air to his lungs and blood to his brain. As he flailed, she tripped him and followed him to the floor, landing on top. Clinically, she listened to his wheezing breaths and felt his labored, panicked pulse. Ace spoke conversationally through her clenched teeth as his struggles ebbed. "Remorse? Strange. I'm not feeling any."

When he went limp, Ace slapped handcuffs on his wrists, pinned the wheel, and slipped away.

Donning her own gas mask, she jogged back to join Bert and Quack as their fizzing canisters sputtered to silence. She gave them the thumbs-up sign and counted to fifty.

Voice muffled by the gas mask, Ace said, "That should be enough time. Careful, now." The trio flitted cautiously belowdecks.

Cabin by cabin, they found no one awake. Not one of the snoring bodies objected as handcuffs snapped closed around their wrists. Ace and her associates expected this docility due to the sleep-inducing gas that filled the ship's atmosphere.

In paradoxical ordinariness, the celebrated Cremona Cannon reclined on a chair in the captain's cabin, safe in its case. As for P. Charles Derkin, one of the cabin doors was locked. The pockets of groggy, handcuffed crew members yielded the needful keys. Derkin lay inside, unconscious but unbruised.

Ace and her associates hauled bodies around for a while. They packed their prisoners into separate cabins and used spare cuffs to chain them to stanchions or bulkheads.

From the moment of boarding, the coup wrapped up in thirty-five minutes. In the wheelhouse, Ace found a radio. She adjusted its frequency to match the one Vivian expected. "Ship secured. I have the helm."

As the sky grew light with approaching dawn, Quack carried coffee service into the wheelhouse, having scrounged for it in the *Tern*'s galley. He joined Bert and Ace and a foggy-headed P. Charles Derkin. Quack chirped, "So, does this make us pirates?"

Bert shot him a sour glare. "No, but if you like, I'll

put your eye out so you can wear an eye patch."

"Two-faced brat," Quack said. "You're awfully mouthy when Miss Rosavino isn't present in the room."

"Isa?" Derkin vigorously rubbed his groggy eyes. "Where is she?"

Bert solemnly pointed upwards. Quack poured coffee for Derkin and amplified, "She is overhead, in the dirigible we chased you in."

Ace left off flipping through the *Tern*'s navigation charts to seize Derkin's wrist. As she stared at her chronometer and counted his pulse, she asked, "Did you hear anyone mention Copenhagen while you were a prisoner?"

Derkin's brow furrowed. "No, not Copenhagen. They called the leader Tim, the one with the British accent. And they mentioned delivering the plans to Darko Dor."

CHAPTER 15

Ace and Quack froze in place and stared at Derkin. Bert choked on his coffee.

He looked from face to face. "Wh-what? What did I say?"

Bert cleared his throat. "It sounded like you said that your captors mentioned *delivering the plans to Darko Dor.*" Intent upon Derkin, the lawyer leaned forward. "Is that what you said?"

"Why, yes!" Derkin's Adam's apple bounced. "That's why we were going so fast. To deliver the plans to Darko Dor. I don't know who that is. I don't know what they meant." The violinist drew himself taller and set his jaw.

Ace found that she still had her fingers on Derkin's wrist, but she had lost count of his pulse. She returned control of the arm to its owner. "The murky depths just got deeper, fellas. Based on these navigation charts, this yacht was likely bound for Copenhagen. And now there are 'plans' and a certain Ottoman we know by the name of Dor."

"Ottoman?" Derkin blinked. "But the war is over. There was an armistice. There were trials."

"Darko Dor was Minister of Technology," Quack said solemnly. "He was never caught, never brought to trial."

"What does it mean?" Derkin said.

"It means two things." Ace flicked gold-flecked

eyes toward the dawn, focused beyond infinity. Then her eagle glance speared toward Derkin. "One, you're lucky to be alive. Darko Dor has no regard for human life. Two, that violin is quite the mystery."

The words hung in the air among the four.

Ace's eyes roved. "We need to get to a telegraph office as soon as possible."

"Where is the nearest one?" Bert said.

"We're closer to Europe than North America now. I'd guess Plymouth, England."

In the wind shadow of Dursey Island on the Irish coast, sheltered from the rolling swells of the Atlantic Ocean, Conall's little boat rode placidly on the glassy sea. The fisherman sat in the stern and coiled his net. As his callused fingers handled the wet rope, he inspected it for damage. Always, something would need repair. The nets, the baskets, the hull, the rigging. It was always something.

But that was the life of the sea, and Conall had been fishing the Irish coast since the days of Queen Elizabeth.[9] Even during the Great War, he had kept at it, six days a week with never a week missed.

Movement caught his rheumy eye, and he speared a narrow gaze southward.

He adjusted his cap against the sparkling sun.

A huge silvery airship hovered over a fast yacht.

---

[9] According to Conall.

Conall's well-creased frown wrinkles deepened. Neither sort of vessel had disturbed Conall's fishing before. Not in all his long years.

In the calm waters and calm atmosphere, the airship descended. Ropes dangled, uncoiling on their way down. Two men on the yacht caught the ends and lashed them taut. A rope ladder tumbled from the gondola as the dirigible strained gently upward, yearning for the skies.

"That's a fret,"[10] grumbled old Conall.

A woman in black climbed down from the airship to the yacht. Once she found the deck, a taller woman climbed up into the silvery gondola. Although both wore something black with trousers instead of a dress, the fisherman wasn't so blind he couldn't judge their gender.

"Quare, sure look it!"[11] Conall's brow furrowed.

The rope ladder ascended, men on deck cut the tethers, and all four airship engines throbbed to life. After it gathered speed, the dirigible raced southeast. The yacht cruised at a more sedate but still rapid speed in roughly the same direction.

Conall shook his shaggy head and returned to stowing his net. "Spies, like as not. I'm not sure I'll ever tell this story. The lads at the pub'll think I'm fibbin'."

---

[10] An Irish expression of disbelief.

[11] Scholars have failed to assign a specific meaning to this Irish phrase (except Irish ones, but they won't share their insights).

Half a day later, the *Tern*'s radio crackled with Ace's voice. "Bert. Set course for Amsterdam. Over."

"Will do, Ace! Any particular reason? Over."

"Sam and Gooper will meet us there, for one. Maybe we can get some police help, for another. And I want to see a doctor. Over."

Bert's eyes flew wide. "A doctor! Are you sick?"

"The doctor is for the Cremona Cannon. I'll explain later. Over and out."

With a click, Ace went off the air. Bert frowned at the softly hissing loudspeaker. "Ace, you drive me a bit crazy. But it's worth it. Just look at me: captain of a yacht! At my tender age, too. Furthermore, I have managed to avoid wrecking her, so far!"

Bert spread his feet wide and lifted his chin. He rested a hand on the wheel like a sea captain of yore. Dappled sunlight blanketed the English Channel, and a modest tailwind pushed the speedy yacht even faster. Isabella Rosavino meandered through the wheelhouse, ruffled Bert's hair, and bumped hips with him. Metal jingled.

His eyebrows shot up, but in the next moment, he triggered his most dashing smile. She smirked at him over her shoulder, then sauntered forward and draped herself decoratively on a deck chair.

Bert's chest swelled, and he proclaimed ebulliently, "It's life at sea for me!" A moment later, his eyes narrowed and roved left and right. "Though with only one woman on the vessel, I'd like to tip a few men overboard. Such as that lout, Quack. All in a spirit of fun, of course."

♠ ♠ ♠

The fair weather turned gloomy by the time the *Tern* arrived at Amsterdam, its cargo of kidnappers surly but intact. Because Bert's and Quack's navigation skills were shaky, the pace of their approach was timid. They were relieved when a tugboat met them and a pilot in a raincoat hopped aboard.

The pipe-smoking and bewhiskered Dutchman spoke English. "Which dock?"

Quack and Bert exchanged glances. "Erm," Quack said, "Amsterdam."

"Ja, and which dock? There are a hundred. And if you don't own it or rent it, you can't tie up."

Bert drew himself up and beamed a brilliant grin. "The police dock, please."

Quack nodded frantically. "The dock nearest the police station, please."

The Dutchman puffed pipe smoke at them. "You have no idea what you are doing."

"It will all work out," Quack assured him. "Trust us."

Grudgingly, the Dutchman steered the *Tern* through the lock and then along miles of canals. The green fields, neatly cobbled streets, and stately architecture of the storied center of commerce glided by under graying skies.

The pilot brought them safely to dock, and Quack and Bert managed to toss rope loops over the pier posts. Grunting with effort, they slid out a gangplank.

When Bert, Quack, Isabella, P. Charles Derkin, and the Cremona Cannon descended the gangplank, Ace awaited them. To Bert and Quack's delight, she wasn't alone. To her right stood a short, rotund, placid man with dark skin and a curled moustache. To her left hulked a figure almost as broad as he was tall, with pale skin, a drooping mustache, and flaming red hair.

"Sam! Gooper!" Quack cried.

They clasped hands in various combinations with great energy. Charles said, "They're either great friends or they're trying to rip each other's arms out of their sockets."

Ace looked upon the scene fondly. "Yes, they are friends, though they pretend otherwise when it suits them. Gooper, Sam, this is P. Charles Derkin and Isabella Rosavino. Charles and Isa, these two are also associates of the detective agency. Come on. Let's go to the police station. We can share news as we walk."

Gooper tipped his bowler hat. "M'lady. Sir."

Sam bowed from his ample waist. "A pleasure."

They strolled together in a group. Ace led. As usual, she seemed to know the way. They stepped away from the docks onto avenues lined with storefronts underneath apartment windows.

"I can't believe I am in Amsterdam!" Isabella kept her hand tucked around P. Charles Derkin's elbow. "May I go shopping?"

"Well, I don't see why not," Charles said. "I'm not kidnapped anymore, and I've been wearing the same suit for days!"

Ace said, "Police first, if you please. The kidnappers should be taken into custody." Her face brightened, and she asked of the group, "Do you know what they call sad thugs in Paris?"

Her associates sent wary glances to each other. Derkin said, "No. What?"

Ace grinned big. "Blue la goons."

The facial expressions of her associates grew strained, like men enduring headaches.

Ace's forehead wrinkled. "Oh, come on, fellas. Where's the love? That was a real whopper."

"Was-a that a joke?" Isa whispered to Charles.

Ace sighed and glanced at the short Egyptian-Chinese man. "Sam? What did you find out in Sögel?"

Sam answered happily with impeccable diction, "A tale to make an archaeologist's heart beat faster, Lady Ace."

"A veritable cascade of idiosyncratic circumstances," added Gooper in a thick Cockney accent.

"Not long ago, a sidewalk in Sögel needed repair." Sam curled the ends of his neat little mustache as he enjoyed his own narration. "The workmen dug down. To their surprise, they found an iron strongbox underneath the cobbles. It was sealed all around in wax to make it waterproof."

Gooper's bushy moustache quivered in excitement as he took up the tale. "The mayor 'imself was called over to examine the enigmatic container. 'E decided it might be a time capsule."

"A time capsule?" Bert said. "Oh, the sort of thing sometimes sealed under a building cornerstone?"

"Yes, Bert," Sam said. "The mayor expected a sampling of letters and newspapers and souvenirs from long ago. But when he and the whole town council opened it, they found both less and more than they expected."

Gooper nodded so fast he almost lost his bowler hat. "There were letters, aye, but not very old. From the early days of the Great War. All the letters were by

Varque d'Rasque, the inventor. You know, the barking mad one."

Quack interjected, "That jogs my memory. I heard stories that this d'Rasque fellow would howl at the moon and work naked and other eccentric things. And that he invented half of the Ottoman war machines. Tanks, planes, bombs, you name it."

"I have heard some of that, too, Quack," Sam said. "But the top letter was not mad. It was very plain. The box contained secrets. Secrets of the inventor that he did not wish the Ottoman Empire to possess. So he buried the box under a construction site. The box, the inventor thought, would be undiscovered for many years."

"How brilliant," said P. Charles Derkin. "His plan worked. The war ended years ago."

Sam traced the curly ends of his mustache with a finger. "Yes, but Varque d'Rasque obscured his secrets even more. After saying, 'These are my inventions I refuse to give to the Ottomans,' the rest is more like a treasure hunt."

"Or a box o' riddles." Gooper blew air through his mustache. "No drawings or diagrams except some maps as clues."

Ace prompted, "And the connection to the Cremona Cannon?"

Sam said, "It was a single sentence, memsahib. No map, nothing. D'Rasque wrote 'The plans for the jet propulsion engine are hidden in the Cremona Cannon' on a page by itself."

"Plans," said Bert.

"Hidden in the Cremona Cannon," Quack said darkly.

"To be delivered to Darko Dor as quickly as possible," Ace ended grimly.

CHAPTER 16

Gooper's eyes popped out. "Wot, now? Darko Dor?"

Ace's mouth pulled to one side in a wry expression. "I'm afraid so. Looks like he hired the gang that kidnapped Derkin and stole the Cremona Cannon. But here's the police station. Let's see if we can get some help."

They marched up some stone steps and under a sign that said "Politie" to find a neat office inside. A few uniformed officers lounged or sauntered among the desks. Ace confidently started up a conversation with the officer sporting the most colorful rank insignia.

Isabella plucked Bert's sleeve. "She speaks Dutch?"

Bert gazed at the raven-haired photographer. "And who-knows-how-many other languages."

"Si. Bella." Isa's brown eyes regarded Ace's profile at length.

Ace's tones of voice became colder. The police officer wrote in a notepad, asking questions in a methodical, plodding way.

P. Charles Derkin set the violin case down. "This is taking a while."

Bert eyed Quack up and down. "It's you. You're all scruffy. You don't look trustworthy."

"Brat," Quack replied sourly.

"Hack."

"Charlatan."

But neither of them could find enthusiasm for their usual game of insult trading as Ace's bitten-off answers grew harsher and her hands balled up into fists.

Finally, Ace turned to them and icily said, "Jurisdiction issues. After all that, the inspector will send two — two! — officers to watch the ship while he makes phone calls to those with the proper authority. Come on."

Ace and the officer exchanged glares, then she about-faced and stalked out of the police station. Helter-skelter, the others regrouped and hurried after.

Bert's gait accelerated to the verge of jogging as he strove to keep up with Ace's long, quick strides. "It shouldn't matter if the police are slow. The ship should be safe. Those handcuffs you ordered were spectacular. Strong. The kidnappers are good and stuck."

Gooper slammed one ham fist into his palm. "Want I should go watch them pestiferous malefactors?"

Ace sighed, and her pace slacked off a trifle. "Bert, you're right. They can't break free without the handcuff key. All the same, Gooper, I'd feel better if you and Sam went back to the *Tern*. Bert and Quack, too, if you don't mind."

Ace stopped at a doorway.

Derkin and the Cremona Cannon nearly bumped into her. "It's a doctor's office," the violinist observed. Carved into stone next to the door, two serpents entwined around a winged staff.

"Aye, that's a caduceus." Gooper smiled serenely. "And, ma'am, we'd be unequivocally euphoric ter surveil yon watercraft."

Bert groaned. "Gooper! Oy!"

Gooper's string of gratuitous whoppers cracked Ace's grim lips into an upward curve. "Good. Go ahead. Isa, Charles, and I will catch up to you as soon as we can."

♠ ♠ ♠

The four associates briskly walked their back trail. The weather deteriorated. Thickening clouds spat rain, and winds gusted. Street merchants shuttled their outdoor displays inside, wearing the fatalistic faces borne of a thousand such soggy interruptions.

Sam's breath came in gusts as he sped his short legs to keep up. "Quack? How did you capture the whole ship? As usual, Lady Ace was short on long tales."

Quack barked a short chuckle. "Oh, we didn't fight fair. We fed ether into the air ducts and put them all to sleep. Ace insisted on adding nitrogen to the ether."

"Yes, she did," Bert said. "Something about preventing the whole ship from exploding, as I recall."

Gooper snorted. "Aye, ether's flammable, all right!"

Sam said, "And what is Lady Ace doing at the doctor's office?"

Quack shook his blond head. "She didn't say, except that it's about the violin, not her."

Bert said, "It's all a riddle right now. The Cremona Cannon is somehow equated with 'plans' that Darko Dor wants. And your recent news, Sam, indicates that the plans are for a— What were those words, again?"

"Jet propulsion engine," Sam supplied.

Quack said, "And what's that?"

"'Jet' is like 'squirt,'" Gooper contributed. "Squids such as *Illex argentinus* get around that way. They inhale water, then squirt it out through a tube called a siphon."

The avenue spat them out canalside.

Bert said doubtfully, "Varque d'Rasque designed a mechanical squid?"

"It is a guess as good as any, Bert," Sam said.

"Are we lost? I don't see the *Tern*," Quack said, squinting through the thickening rain.

"Hey!" Bert exclaimed, pointing toward another berth. "It's the monocle man!"

Indeed, it was. The proper and officious Filbert Monocles descended the gangplank of a small cruise ship. He wore a suit and sheltered under a black umbrella. Four sturdy men followed him, each with their own umbrella.

Monocles spotted Bert and Quack and raised a finger in their direction. His reedy tenor called sharply, "You, there!"

"He's in the organization that rents out the violin," Quack said. "But what's he doing here?"

Bert muttered, "And right now, too. This can't be a coincidence."

Monocles arrived, fished out his monocle, and squeezed it into his eye socket. He peered at Bert and Quack, one pupil magnified. "Good day to you! I am Filbert Monocles of the International Society for the Preservation of Historic Artifacts."

"We recall," Bert said. "I am Hubert Bostock. This is Sam Biming, Phileas Locknard, and Warburton

Snana. Fancy us meeting here, like this, eh?"

Monocles shrugged off the suspicious tone. "The Derkin kidnapping is an international sensation. I called your New York office, and they sent me here. Can you tell me the news? The New York receptionist was curt. And uninformative."

The four associates exchanged glances and shrugs. Sam answered, "I think there is no need to keep secrets. We have recovered P. Charles Derkin and his violin."

Monocles stood straighter, and his permanent expression of disapproval evaporated. "That is good news. Where are they, might I ask?"

Rapid footsteps clattered. Two Dutch policemen ran by, going from the direction of the docked *Tern* back toward the police station.

"I say!" Monocles complained at the interruption.

The four associates squinted at the retreating backs of the officers, finding the sight unsettling somehow. The two officers skirted three familiar figures that approached through the curtain of rain.

Quack said, "If I'm not mistaken, here comes Derkin right now."

"Wait. Why were those policemen running?" Bert said.

"The kidnappers escaped?" Sam wondered.

The other three associates stared at Sam. The footsteps of Ace, Isa, and Derkin clattered toward them, suddenly at a run.

"Come on!" Gooper howled and lumbered toward the dock. He accelerated to a rumbling gallop.

Everyone followed Gooper's lead, even, after a few moments, Filbert Monocles and his four assistants.

"What? Wait! Stop!" cried Monocles. The pane of glass popped from his eye socket to dangle on a fine chain as he gave undignified chase.

The scene clarified soon.

The dock lay completely empty except for the chopped-off ends of mooring ropes. The *Tern* had vanished.

Ace groaned. She scanned the docks and saw only barges, freighters, and the cruise ship in which Monocles had come. "They've escaped. And not a fast boat in sight! They'll be through the lock and into the North Sea in minutes."

"Where's the airship?" Bert asked breathlessly.

Ace's teeth clenched. "Miles away. At the airport."

"Can the police order the lock closed?" Sam asked.

Charles Derkin laughed as he arrived. "I'm going to come away from this adventure quite fit. That is, if I don't catch my death from this chill rain."

"I can't think of how to chase down the *Tern* in time," Ace said. "No boat fast enough nearby. Can't swim after it. Sam's car isn't near enough. I can't think of any Dutch friends to call. Hopefully, the police will act faster than they have so far."

Filbert Monocles clattered to a stop as he joined the group. His breath whistled as his sharp voice rapped out, "Mister Derkin."

"Monocles?" Derkin's eyebrows shot upward.

"Mr. Derkin. In accordance with clause twelve, subsection *b*, I hereby reclaim the Cremona Cannon."

CHAPTER 17

Everyone stared at the fellow. Only the patter of rain could be heard until Monocles drew himself up to full height and inserted his monocle. "It is all correct and proper. The ISPHA can reclaim an instrument in extraordinary circumstances. This business of kidnapping and transatlantic chases certainly qualifies."

"Oh, Charles!" Isabella gasped.

P. Charles Derkin exhaled, blowing out his cheeks. "Well, it's a shock. But, honestly, I'm a bit sick of the whole thing. I'd rather put it all behind me."

"Very sensible," Monocles said, extending his hand.

Derkin placed the handle of the violin case in the hand of the suited man.

"Wait," Ace said.

Her four associates fanned out behind her. Symmetrically, the four silent men that Monocles brought fanned out behind him.

"Why?" Filbert Monocles examined the tall, golden-skinned woman dressed in a simple flight suit.

"There are things you don't know. It's much more serious than you imagine," Ace said.

Monocles seemed less than impressed. "Be brief."

"The international criminal Darko Dor thinks that there are technical plans hidden in the violin. Specifically, a secret invention of Varque d'Rasque that he believes will aid his ambitions. He wants to obtain the violin and disassemble it to find the blueprints."

"Frankly, that sounds insane." The displeased lines

between Monocles's graying brows deepened.

"Not so insane. Darko Dor's efforts started small, but now he expends more and more effort. At first, he hired only a person or two to scare Derkin into giving the violin away or, at least, leaving it unguarded. Partly due to luck, the violin was never left unguarded long enough for them to act. When that failed, they sent a gang of heavies to take it. They almost succeeded the first time. They did succeed the second time, though we managed to rescue Derkin and the Cannon."

Monocles frowned, but in a thoughtful way, not a stubborn way. "Why does Dor want it now, all of a sudden?"

The adventuress said, "He has sought it ever since he heard about the jet engine plans. That dates to when the cache of the inventor's materials was uncovered in Sögel. Shortly after that, Thorpe G. Scott died in a freak accident."

"Ah," Monocles said.

"ISPHA recovered the violin from Scott's safe, then gave it to Ekaterina Brusikova. I note that the safe in question is extremely heavy and very secure."

"And Brusikova also had an accident," Monocles said, his Adam's apple bouncing.

"No," Ace corrected. "It was murder. She was thrown from her window to her death. The police do not know who pushed her out. Now, allow me a speculation. In the case of Brusikova, I guess that ISPHA recovered the violin within hours, or even minutes, after her death."

"Eh, yes. She was about to tour in Russia. Our people—" Monocles glanced at the silent men flanking him "—were nearby."

Ace said, "As I surmised. I think, given a little more time, Dor's agents would have hauled the safe away."

"The violin went to P. Charles Derkin next." Monocles ran a finger around his collar, as if the collar was now too tight.

"Yes, and he was soon pestered with phone calls and visitors, all angling to separate him from the violin. Not to mention the haunting. But now, all of that seems trivial. Darko Dor wants the violin, and he wants it badly." Ace leaned forward and locked eyes with the diminutive official. "You should not take it, Mr. Monocles. The location of your headquarters is known. Darko Dor will have it, no matter the obstacle."

Monocles straightened to his full height, sufficient to look Ace in the throat. "Ridiculous. Our security is excellent. Besides, what is the alternative? To give it to you? Preposterous."

"Maybe us. Better us than you because we're sneakier. I do not covet the violin. I'm a pianist, not a violinist." Ace examined his stony countenance then added a final plea. "Please. Darko Dor is … well, he's evil."

Monocles was no longer listening. "Many artifacts are entrusted to our care, Miss Carroway. One more item is not a concern. If that is all, I bid you all a good day." He curtly bowed, then pivoted on his heel to face Derkin. "I do apologize, Mr. Derkin. I did not dream you were in such danger. But now it is over. Farewell."

"Oh. Yes. Goodbye," Derkin said with a vague wave.

The party of five from ISPHA and their umbrellas receded until they blended with the gray curtain of rain and disappeared.

The rest stood in the downpour with slumped shoulders, getting soaked.

Quack's voice came, mournful and low. "We've lost the violin, and we've lost the trail of the crooks, too."

CHAPTER 18

The hum of the airship engines permeated the gondola. Bert twiddled his thumbs in the control room, watching Gilbert master the helm. Despite his youth (Bert wondered if he was old enough to vote), the clean-cut young man controlled *Sky Arrow One* with imperturbable calm. They flew blind. Clouds filled the skies, and a peppering of water droplets splattered and ran in rivulets down the control room windows. The airship cruised somewhere over the North Sea.

Bert's eyes roved to the coffeepot. "I could do with a cup of joe."

"Five cents, please," said Gilbert.

"What?" Bert's hand stopped in its motion.

"Vivian is in charge of the coffee, and she said she is happy to provide it, but that coffee isn't free."

The Boston lawyer scrunched his face up. "She is both absolutely correct and horribly cruel."

"Yes, sir, that's Vivian."

Bert patted his pockets. Nothing jingled.

He blinked, and his breath caught in his throat. His eyes widened. He patted again. Still no jingle.

Slumping forward, he hung his head and groaned.

"Mr. Bostock?" queried Gilbert.

The lawyer squinted up at the helmsman. "I just realized I'm a heel, that's all. Carry on." Bert rose from his chair and slunk into the lounge.

By the portside windows, Isabella and Derkin leaned on each other and watched the wisps of gray whisk by. The sight did nothing to erase the pained expression from Bert's face. He crept by them to get aft to the double row of cabin doors.

He knocked on Ace's. A familiar alto responded through the metal. "Come!"

Inside, at the fold-down desk, a figure hunched. With a magnifying glass, Ace pored over a twelve-by-twelve-inch glass plate. She glanced up and over. "Hello, Bert."

"Ace. I'm a fool. Uh. What is that?" Bert squinted at the photographic plate. It was dominated by a bright square in the middle of a black background, but on the black were faint gray curves in the shape of … "A violin?"

"It is an X-ray image of the Cremona Cannon and my reason for going to the doctor's office in Amsterdam. Why do you say you're a fool, Bert?"

Bert wrung his hands. "I don't have my handcuff key, Ace! It's not in my pocket. I don't know when I lost it, but it looks like I did."

Ace's eyebrows rose in inquiry. "So?"

"So I'm the reason the prisoners escaped and sailed away!"

Ace shrugged. "It's all right, Bert. Really. Remember, we tried questioning them and got nowhere, even with gap-toothed Tim. I thought we might jar something out of him since we knew his name, but no."

"No. He just snarled like a rabid wolf."

"Just so. But even if the ship and men had been impounded by the police, it wouldn't slow Darko Dor down much."

The corners of Bert's mouth twitched downward, then hesitantly upward. "I suppose we still rescued

Derkin and his violin."

"That's right. See? Victory is ours. Now, come here. I want to show you this X-ray. What do you suppose the bright rectangle is?" Ace carefully failed to touch the glass of the photographic plate when she pointed.

"Erm, no idea. Do violins have hard rectangles inside them?"

"No, they shouldn't. But this one does. It appears to be a very thin metal foil, carefully inlaid into the back of the violin. One notable consequence is that, since the back of the violin is curved, the foil acts like a parabolic reflector."

Bert's expression was blank.

The outside corners of Ace's eyes squeezed in amusement at his reaction. "A reflector and amplifier for something like, say, a pulse transmitter stuffed into the violin case."

"Knock me over with a feather!" Bert's eyebrows shot up. "So when we first picked up the pulses, they were amplified because of the foil?"

"Yes. Vivian suggested something like it at the time. She set me thinking that I'd like to take an X-ray photograph of the violin. And, pardon me if I toot my own horn, but taking an X-ray was a really good idea. Take a closer look. Don't touch."

Bert bent closer to the bright rectangle, finally seeing faint, fine lines traced across it. He blinked. He whistled, long and slow. "It's a blueprint. And a lot of algebra symbols."

"Yes. It's even got a signature. Varque d'Rasque, as you'd expect. I haven't quite understood the algebra. It's leading me toward some fairly obscure thermodynamics. But I think I understand the basic idea." Ace's half smile was the only outward clue of her quiet triumph.

"Would I understand it?" Bert wondered wryly.

"Of course. It's an airplane engine with the propeller inside a tube. The tube narrows and focuses the airflow. I'm betting that increases the thrust of the engine."

"More thrust is good, right?"

"Right." Ace pointed to the diagram with the tip of a pen. "The oddest part is that there is no motor to spin the propeller. But to the rear of the blades, fuel is squirted in. I'm starting to think the gas is ignited there. Flame shoots out the rear, and some vanes catch that exhaust to power the propeller. That's revolutionary, Bert. It might be ten times more powerful than what we've got now."

"A more powerful airplane engine. All right, I get it." Bert's pleased expression ended in an abrupt frown. "Ace! We've got to make sure Darko Dor doesn't get his hands on this!"

"You can say that again."

The air voyage did not last long. Everyone clumped into the control room as they descended. Ace said from her position at the helm of *Sky Arrow One*, "We've two reasons to go to Copenhagen. The *Tern* was going there, and ISPHA headquarters is there."

"Could Copenhagen," mused Bert, "be a hideout for Dor's crime operations?"

"Possibly so. We'd better watch our step. Darko Dor might have a whole organization set up here."

"Wicked good." An eager light shone in Bert's eye. "I still owe somebody for that wallop on my temple."

Night had fallen, but the clouds were breaking up. The lights of Copenhagen shone magically on gargoyles and dragons made of mist as the *Sky Arrow* descended.

Quack communicated by radio with the airport, telling outrageous fibs. "Emergency landing for repairs, tower. Over."

P. Charles Derkin pointed out the window. "That moat is shaped like a star!"

"It is the Citadel of Copenhagen," Isabella said. "There were once many star fortresses, built centuries ago. This one is preserved well."

"You know Copenhagen?" Derkin said.

Isabella nodded. "I have visited as a tourist, yes. Look, there. A large fountain. A goddess driving oxen."

"The Norse goddess Gefion," Sam said. "Swedish king Gylfi granted a merry wandering woman as much land as she could plow in a day and a night. But the woman was a goddess of Asgard who transformed her four sons into enormous oxen. They carved out a portion of Sweden and dragged it to Denmark to become the land known as Zealand, this large island where Copenhagen sits."

"I love travelling with Sam," Bert said.

"Do you need assistance? Over," crackled the radio speaker.

"Tell them we're landing at the Citadel to make repairs," Ace said, cutting power to the engines and settling lower.

"Negative, tower. We have a landing area. On the grounds of the Citadel. Over," Quack spoke into the microphone somewhat gleefully.

"Kastellet?" The crackly voice seemed alarmed.

"Tell them yes," Ace instructed Quack. "There. Between the windmill and the church. Nicely surrounded by trees. Quite obscured from view from the harbor direction."

"Yes. Over," Quack said.

Sky Arrow One set down on grass, light as a feather at first, then more and more firmly as compressors emptied lifting gas from the bladders and stored it in metal tanks.

"Right," said Ace. "Vivian and Gilbert, set out the usual gawker fence. I don't think there's anything to do tonight but sleep. Tomorrow, we'll get busy."

CHAPTER 19

Isabella eyed the light that shone in the crack under Ace's cabin door. She arranged her hair about her shoulders before she knocked.

"Come in," Ace called.

Raven hair, dark eyes, and a teasing smile posed in the doorway. "You and I, we do not sleep yet. What do you do, in this hour when only owls should be awake?"

Ace straightened up from the tiny metal desk and stretched, chuckling. "Do you really want to know?" The X-ray of the violin was propped up with an electric light behind it. Paper covered in equations littered the desktop.

"Yes, yes. I asked, *sì?*"

"You did ask." Ace nibbled at her pencil eraser. "I'm trying to remember some obscure physics. I think I recall enough to at least sort out the symbols d'Rasque used."

"*Incredibile!* I did not get a good look until now." Isabella pushed off the doorway and drifted into the cabin. She rested hands on Ace's shoulders and bent to examine the X-ray. "And you say you understand this? I think I understand the picture only."

"No, I don't understand his new physics, yet, but I

know what he's attempting. He's trying to quantify the forward thrust from this jet engine in terms of thermodynamic quantities. It's just rare stuff: enthalpy, entropy, and free energy ..." Ace's eyes swiveled to find Isabella's very near.

"But you have remembered. You will solve it," Isabella said softly.

"Erm. Well, I ..."

"Shy again. You amaze me, Ace. Never have I met a one like you. Your words, your actions, they are in accord. The rest of us, we lie all the time. To others. To ourselves." A ghost of pain crossed Isa's face to be replaced with a glow of admiration. "Not you. Not you."

Ace dropped her golden gaze. "Erm. Would you like some herbal tea? I hear it helps to fall asleep."

Isabella laughed and gave Ace's shoulders a squeeze. "But of course! I will not embarrass you more. We can have tea, and we can talk of airplanes and jet engines."

"That's risky. Airplanes are my favorite topic."

"I like risk."

In the morning, Filbert Monocles arrived at the gates to ISPHA late and tired. While he never became overtly seasick, he did find it difficult to sleep aboard a rolling ship. The guard checked his badge and waved him through. He barely noticed the manicured gardens or the seventeenth-century stonework of the ISPHA building.

His gloomy mood darkened further when he breached his outer office to find a row of composed, determined faces waiting.

"Good day!" he snapped, fishing his monocle from his vest pocket. For a moment, he glared accusingly at the secretary, who abruptly busied himself with shuffling papers.

Ace took point, flanked by Gooper, Sam, Isabella Rosavino, and P. Charles Derkin. As if continuing the conversation from Amsterdam, she said, "Please reconsider, Mr. Monocles. Darko Dor is an international criminal. I have brought a dossier on him. All his verified exploits are described. You will find it disturbing reading."

Monocles waved away the manila folder that Ace extended. "I don't need that. My decision stands. It would take, I don't know, an army regiment or something to get into our vaults. The violin is safe."

Ace breathed a calming Wing Chun cycle. "I am afraid people will die, Mr. Monocles. I can testify to the single-mindedness of Darko Dor's obsessions. He is not a man one can call sane."

"Sane? Well, I am sane. You people, well, I have doubts." He stabbed a finger in the direction of the exit. "Leave now, please. I do not wish to begin shouting or calling for the guards. My answer stands, I tell you!"

His poised finger trembled. The tension in the room turned the air to fragile glass ready to shatter.

Ace pressed her palms together. "I am sorry you feel this way. If there is no changing your mind, we will go."

In a parody of politeness, Filbert Monocles held the door for them as they exited.

They dragged their way outside, heads down. The noon sun appeared and disappeared behind an array of fleecy clouds. After they passed the last checkpoint, Gooper rumbled, "'Ow was me actin'?"

"Quack would be proud, Gooper," Ace assured him.

He blew air through his bright red mustache. "Good. You don't know how close I was to tacklin' the nearsighted little blighter."

Ace pursed her lips. "I think we made our displeasure evident. A physical assault would have been overkill. And, not to be a mother hen or anything, but we can't really operate from inside the jail." She winked at Gooper.

He grinned back.

Sam furrowed his brow. "Do you think they will notice that seven of us went in, but only five came out?"

Satisfaction dripped from Ace's reply. "Even if they do, they are too late. Quack and Bert should be tucked out of sight by now."

Derkin chuckled. "I quite like all this cloak-and-dagger trickery. I feel positively energized."

"I'll let you know if we have any openings at the agency," Ace said drily.

Derkin laughed. "No, don't take me seriously. I'm a violinist, not a spy."

Ace surveyed her crew. "Isa? Charles? You two made wonderful camouflage just now, but I think it's time to tuck you out of harm's way. Any objection to staying in a hotel for a night or two until things clarify?"

Isabella and Charles Derkin looked at each other. Isabella smiled rakishly. Charles stuttered, "N-no objection!"

At luncheon, Ace got wind of a nearby shop that rented motorcycles. The party rented two, with sidecars. The Hotel Gefion provided adjoining rooms for P. Charles Derkin and Isabella Rosavino. By mid-afternoon, Gooper, Sam, and Ace zoomed away through Copenhagen on the pair of motorcycles. Ace resembled a racer in her aviator goggles and scarf. Sam carried his innate dignity to the ride, head high and back straight. Gooper, however, hulked awkwardly in Sam's sidecar. He leaned forward with reddened face, his flowing mustache flying backwards. His ham hands gripped the edges of his capsule. "I do *not* trust this knavish contraption."

Fortunately for Gooper, distances in Copenhagen were short. *Sky Arrow One*, Hotel Gefion, and the ISPHA building were all within a half mile of each other. The airship entertained a steady stream of curiosity seekers. Ace, Sam, and Gooper threaded through clumps of gawkers to check in with Gilbert and Vivian.

The teens reported all quiet. When Ace left, she stowed a suitcase radio in her sidecar. Gooper stowed cloth-wrapped bundles into the sidecars and hung field glasses around his bulky neck.

After a motorcycle scouting tour, the trio selected a hidden nook off to the side of the walled ISPHA grounds. A convenient tree would let them peek over the wall without becoming visible to the guard shack. Ace remarked in vexed tones, "I don't think there is anybody on guard outside. The gatehouse is empty."

"Perhaps there will be patrols, memsahib."

"I hope so. The place is wide open otherwise."

They warmed up the suitcase radio as the sun set.

Bert answered immediately. "All quiet, Ace. I am hidden up in the attic. Nobody's around to hear me. They all went home a couple of hours ago. Quack's mopping floors, I think. Brilliant disguise, the custodian outfit, but it has a downside, ha, ha! Uh, over."

"Do you know where the Cremona Cannon is? Over."

"Oh, sure. It's on the ground level. There's a great, big vault down there. Huge. It holds all kinds of things. Books, statues, paintings. Even a mummy. The door is all locked up now, and there are four guards. Uh, over."

"Are the guards armed? Over."

"Sidearms, yes. Over."

"Good work, Bert. We'll check in again in one hour. Over."

"One hour, on the dot. Over and out, Ace."

CHAPTER 20

P. Charles Derkin retreated to his room. Isabella had had some trouble with getting her room telephone connected. Derkin could think of phone calls he should make, too, but he just flopped on the bed and closed his eyes.

Half dreaming of dark, flashing eyes, he heard Isabella's door close. She must be back. The walls must be thin.

"'Allo? 'Allo? Yes. Danzig, please. Zero four five one."

Charles's lips curled in a smile as Isabella's voice came, faint but clear, from the next room.

"I will wait."

Charles brought a finger to his lips, brushing them softly. His smile turned wistful but also curved in anticipation. Who knew what this night might bring?

"'Allo? Yes. This is Scarab."

His daydream fizzled. Scarab?

Isabella intoned, "Time eight. Time one. Time zero," as if reciting by rote.

The violinist wrinkled his nose, then closed his eyes, determined to catnap.

"I will wait."

Charles twitched. He opened his eyes and frowned. Finally, he reached for the pad of paper and pencil stub on the nightstand.

"'Allo? I speak to Mongoose himself? It is an honor, your Excellency."

"Time one time zero," scribbled Charles.

"Yes, Lord Dor, I have good news."

Charles's pencil froze. Had Isabella said "Lord Dor"?

"Carroway had an X-ray picture of the violin made. I have it. I think it shows what you wanted."

Charles forced his pencil to move: "Scarab. Mongoose, his Excellency, Lord Dor."

"Yes, I can meet a ship."

"X-ray stolen. Ship." Beads of sweat appeared on Charles's forehead.

"Indiagade?[12] Wait, let me confirm. I go to the end of Indiagade, and there is a large boathouse. Yes. Is that all?"

"Indiagade. Boathouse," wrote Charles.

"I shall give that password. Thank you, Your Excellency!"

"What password?" muttered Charles under his breath.

There was a faint "snick" sound from the other side of the thin wall. Charles's face went from pale to flushed. His fists clenched as he levered himself off the bed and stalked toward the door.

At the door, he stopped. He reversed course and plucked his scrap of paper from the bedside table. He stuffed it into his pants pocket and marched back to the door.

He stopped again as lines creased between his eyebrows. Deliberately, he removed his shoe and stuffed

---

[12] Danish: "Gade" is "street."

his note into the toe of it. The latch next door rattled. He hastily jammed his foot back into his shoe and tied a speedy tangle with the laces. He leaped out into the hallway.

"Isa!"

From fifteen feet down the hall, she turned. Her alarmed face relaxed to an easy smile. "Darling, do pardon me. I'm still having telephone trouble. I'll be back shortly."

"You," said Charles unsteadily, "have Miss Carroway's X-ray in that valise."

Isabella's eyes flashed. She lifted her chin. "What nonsense. Come. Come into my room and I will show you." Isabella marched by Charles with a look of challenge and stormed into her room.

"Yes. Show me. I heard a lot just now!" Charles followed her in.

Isabella flopped her case on the bed, commanding, "Go on! Open it! The joke is on you! It was all a joke, you silly Canadian!"

"A ... a joke? R-really?" Charles went from flushed to pale again. He hunched over the valise and opened it. He caught sight of something square and flat, wrapped in women's undergarments.

With his attention thus directed, Isa clasped her hands together to make a club and swung them against his jaw. A starburst of pain half-blinded him.

CHAPTER 21

Bert yawned.

He muttered, "I wish Quack were up here so I could insult him."

He blearily checked his watch. "Only 12:30? Feels like 4 a.m."

Bert felt a vibration come through the floor, like the slam of a heavy door. For a long minute, he listened, but it did not repeat. He sighed heavily and stretched his limbs. "Well, I'll take another walk, then. I have the whole building to myself, except the ground floor where the highly trained and professional guards are sleeping on the job." He grinned to himself.

In previous excursions, Bert learned that he had free rein over the top two floors and the attic level as well. The only floor with guards and alarms was the ground floor. Quack had checked in with him several times from near the guard station. They had agreed that each would radio the other if anything happened.

The building was lit only by tiny electric safety lights. Bert barely noticed them until, as he emerged from the attic into the stairwell, they all went out.

Bert froze. He was utterly blind. The vibration he had felt earlier returned, stronger. He began feeling his way down to the next level, the second story. A muted, grating crash sounded from outside, toward the rear of the building. He found the landing and skittered out of the stairwell into the corridors. Wan light diffused in from windows at the front and rear of the building.

At a run, he followed his ears to the rear window. His gaze roved out. Motion below directed his eyes down to a moving bulldozer. In the next instant, the machine plowed into the ground floor wall almost directly below him. The impact shook the building and knocked Bert to his knees. The iron blade cut through the wall as if it were paper. A truck and a smaller vehicle followed the bulldozer.

Gears clashed, but Bert did not stay to watch the bulldozer back out.

He ran back to the stairwell. Risking shins and ankles at the very least, Bert pelted down the inky black stairs, counting the reversals.

As he reached the ground floor, faint light wavered at the stairwell exit. The guard station and vault entrance lay straight ahead, and he could see all four guards. By the light of electric torches, they spun the wheel that retracted the bars holding the vault door shut. As Bert looked on, chewing on his lower lip, they heaved the vault open.

The ponderous door swung. A brighter light burned behind it, from inside the vault room where one might expect only darkness. Bert's eyes widened. The opening door revealed silhouettes of gunmen in wait. Bert whipped back into the stairwell as machine guns roared. Bullets ripped and shredded the doorway to the stairs. Screams of men rang out, only to fall silent a moment later as the brutal fusillade continued.

Bert huddled out of sight, heart pounding. "They just bulldozed their way into the back of the vault! They're more like infantrymen than cat burglars."

The hail of bullets stopped.

"Fear," a male voice said over the ringing in Bert's ears. It took Bert a moment to realize that he probably meant "vier," German for "four." The voice continued, "Das ist alles."[13]

Bert peeked. Light spilled bright from the open vault door. Crumpled bodies lay. Between their long shadows, floodlights reflected upon pools of blood on the floor. Bert's guts churned. The silhouettes of three infantrymen stood over the bodies and searched for more people to shoot. Beyond them, Bert had an impression of industrious comings and goings. Purposeful limbs occasionally blocked the brilliant light sources.

Bert saw no way forward. Charging down the bare hallway toward the gunmen would be suicide. "Where's Quack?" he muttered as he retreated into the stairwell to climb up a level.

He heard a call of "Rückzug!"[14] as he felt his way out of the stairwell again, this time one floor up. The main entrance was on this level, but he skittered the opposite way, to the back of the building. There was a window there, and its glass had shattered out.

Bert cautiously stuck his head out. The bulldozer sat angled off to the side, inert. The big truck's engine roared, and it pulled forward, leaving ISPHA. The third vehicle was a military truck with a machine gun mounted on the back, though a tarp currently obscured its wicked outlines. It followed the truck through a bulldozed gap in a stone wall; a wall that had failed in its duty. A pair of rearguard gunmen swung

---

[13] "That is all [of them]."
[14] "Retreat!"

up to man the machine gun. The convoy of two accelerated, abandoning the bulldozer.

Bert didn't register much of that, though. He was too busy watching Quack. Still dressed as a janitor, the actor clung to the top of the truck, on his belly. Quack spotted Bert and gave him a thumbs-up sign as the truck pulled away.

Bert shook a fist at the receding vehicles. "Cheeky scene-stealer!"

After kicking out some shards of glass, he clambered out the window. Sufficient ledge existed for Bert to sidle along until he was over the bulldozer. Bert jumped. His aim was good. He hit the seat cushion. His bounce was less graceful. He tumbled painfully off the tractor treads and spun to the ground.

With a groan, he picked himself up and lurched after the vehicles, sprinting as best he could manage. As he left the ISPHA grounds and spilled out into the streets of Copenhagen, new roars assaulted his ears, very close. He tensed as he sensed movement behind him, but no bullets followed.

It was a pair of motorcycles. Sam and Gooper waved as they passed him, but Ace screeched to a halt and pointed to her sidecar. Bert hopped in, and Ace peeled out.

"Ace! Good timing! Quack stowed away on the big truck!" Bert panted as speed picked up.

Ace said over the rush of air, "I saw. We were too far away and, honestly, too surprised to help. Also, they were quick! What was that, four and a half minutes total?"

They raced on, soon catching sight of Sam and Gooper's motorcycle and the gun wagon. The men on the small truck were stripping away the canvas covering over an ugly military-grade machine gun.

Gooper held a stubby rifle. He aimed and popped off several rounds.

"What's Gooper got?" Bert asked.

"The mercy slug rifle," Ace replied. "There's another one at your feet, you might like to know." Ace had invented a rifle cartridge that was hollow, containing doses of liquid tranquilizer. Death was far less likely with such bullets.

"Oh. I thought that was my bad ankle acting up." Bert grinned, fishing it out.

"You have a bad ankle?"

"No. Actually, I'm perfect."

Ace snorted.

Gooper whooped as one of the men on the gun wagon cried out and tumbled off. The motorcycles zoomed past the fellow, even as he still rolled over and over on the street.

The machine gun spoke. Heavy bullets tore through the air, splintering cobblestones.

The driver of the gun wagon braked hard. Stone walls hemmed in the narrow street. The motorcycles raced at full speed right into the spray of bullets.

CHAPTER 22

P. Charles Derkin sluggishly groped back to consciousness. His head throbbed. He touched fingers to his temple, and it felt sticky. He groaned and tottered to his feet. "Where am I?"

He stood in a hotel room, but the floor was cluttered. Chairs and lamps lay toppled, and even the desk was askew. He blearily staggered into the bathroom and gasped at his reflection. "Egad. I'm a nightmare." He groaned. Half his face was covered in dried or drying blood. He ran some water and soaked a towel.

As the water cooled his face, full awareness returned. Sharp lances of pain mixed with duller complaints of mere bruises. "No," he muttered. "I'm not a nightmare, I'm *in* a nightmare!" He remembered Isabella hitting him repeatedly, even though he tried to defend himself. He was bounced around the room, unable to counter her precise punches. At last, he slipped and hit his head on the radiator, and knew no more.

"It's not a large cut, after all," he said, inspecting his gashed forehead. He couldn't do anything about the wound itself or his bloody collar, but at least his face was the color of skin again, albeit slightly pale. He didn't feather his damp hair into its usual pompadour. Instead, he pushed it forward until it covered his livid forehead cut.

"Well, Derkin, are you a man or a muskrat? Isabella

141

stole the jet engine plans, and no one knows but you." Derkin straightened to his full height. He took off his shoe, recovered his scribbled note, and read aloud, "Indiagade." His jaw muscles rippled. "I know. I'll stop the ship."

Resolutely, he strode out.

The bellhop stared at him when he asked for directions to Indiagade. Derkin glared back until he got an answer. On the street outside, Derkin muttered, "None of his business if I'm worse for wear. I just wish it was for a better reason. Talk about a romance gone sour!"

Derkin prowled the silent streets. The throbbing in his head eased somewhat as his body limbered up. He kept up an exaggerated stealthiness, whisking from shadow to shadow, even though there wasn't a soul about this late at night.

Light mists rose off the harbor as the violinist came to the end of Indiagade. It ended at the waters of the sound. A pair of piers jutted onto the dark waters, with curved supports arching over them. The top half of the affair was covered in canvas, giving the overall impression of a Conestoga wagon or a giant straight white caterpillar. A big gray ship docked inside. The canvas curtains at the ends seemed designed to hide the ship from view, but at the moment, they were flayed wide open, revealing all. A fence surrounded the facility, but its wide gate also lay fully open.

Derkin flitted closer, using the shrubbery of the last few houses to move unseen. "I wonder if it's a charter ship. Maybe all I have to do is speak with the captain. On the other hand, it might be the property of Darko Dor stem to stern. I'd better be careful."

Derkin skulked like a cinema spy. He nipped inside the fence and hid behind a crate. Stealthily, he peeked. Two men smoked cigarettes and talked in a language Derkin did not know.

Wondering at his own sanity, he tiptoed down the far side of a row of crates stacked on the pier. Halfway down the pier, he peeked again. Nobody. The coast was clear.

Drawing a deep breath, he sprinted and leapt, landing lightly on the deck of the ship. Seeing a blob of black canvas amidships, he veered toward it. He wormed underneath, pulled his legs in, and listened, trying not to breathe.

The voices of the two smokers droned on. Derkin could see only the vaguest of shapes, it was so black under the canvas. He could touch only cold metal. He closed his eyes completely.

Suddenly, Isabella's voice called, only yards away, "Wann fahren wir?" Derkin only barely choked back a shout. Eyes popped wide in the darkness, he shivered.

"Bald. Bald," answered one of the men.

Derkin heard a faint clash of gears and the approaching growl of a large engine.

One of the men laughed. "Ja. Ser bald!"[15]

Footsteps slapped by his hiding place as his throat seemed to choke itself.

He opened his eyes. Adjusted to the darkness, his eyes reported curves and angles. He touched heavy steel. Following the curves sternward, he saw a long metal tube. Ceasing to breathe at all, he recognized it: a

---

[15] The conversation was in German. "When do we leave?" "Soon. Soon." "Yes. Very soon!"

military cannon, very modern, one that hurtled explosive shells.

His throat tightened so much he could not breathe. This was no chartered cruiser.

The ship engines rumbled to life. Panic gripped the violinist.

CHAPTER 23

Sam braked hard as bullets chewed up cobblestones just in front of the speeding motorcycle. Gooper held on for dear life, his muscles bunching as he gripped the sidecar. Veering right, Sam felt the motorcycle itself shudder with impacts. The front tire exploded in fragments of hot rubber.

"Ow!" complained Gooper as the motorcycle bounced up on the sidewalk curb and smacked into the stone wall. Sam, meanwhile, abandoned ship. He let go of the handlebars and leaped straight up in the air. His momentum carried his lower half into the wall, though his top half managed to clear it. The uneven collision made him flip over the wall, feet over head.

Gooper ducked lower as the motorcycle and sidecar clashed with immovable stones. The impact crumpled metal. Despite his death grip on the sidecar, Gooper was torn free and ended up in a heap on the sidewalk.

The deadly hail of bullets spat again, this time at Ace and Bert. Gooper lifted his head and focused bleary eyes. Ace grazed the motorcycle on the curb, bouncing the sidecar and Bert high. Canted over at this steep angle, Ace did the counterintuitive, steering toward the sidecar to keep the sidecar suspended in the air.

With a splintering crunch and a shower of wood fragments, the motorcycle and sidecar blew through a narrow wooden garden gate. It cleared the stony fenceposts only because the sidecar was tipped up.

"Ho! Wot a pulchritudinous trajectory!" Gooper crowed. In the next instant, Gooper threw himself flat behind the sidecar as more hot lead spewed his way, peppering the motorcycle with destruction. The other tire blew. When the volley was done, a gasoline fire burned in the sad remains of what had shortly before been a serviceable motorcycle.

The gun wagon's engine roared. It zoomed away. Light blinked on in every house on the block. Somewhere in Copenhagen, a switchboard operator became very, very busy.

Gooper levered himself to his feet and peeked over the wall. "Sam?"

Sam's voice shakily replied, "Sahib. I am functional, for suitably lenient definitions of 'functional.'"

Bert wobbled past the shattered garden gate and called, "All right over there?"

Gooper waved. "All roight! A few contusions."

Sam limped out of a neat, narrow gate into the street. He glanced gloomily at the burning motorcycle. "Sahib, our transportation is inoperable."

Ace appeared, pushing her motorcycle, sans sidecar. She examined her associates critically. "Not too much blood. We got lucky." They all sported ripped clothing and freely bleeding creases where bullets or shrapnel had sliced, but no wound was deep.

"Lucky? Cor, 'e couldn't shoot 'is way out've a soap bubble," proclaimed Gooper.

Ace snorted. "Right. Get to the airship and get airborne. Quack is wearing a pulse transmitter." She jumped on the starter, and the motorcycle revved.

They watched Ace speed away with looks of envy.

They heaved resigned sighs then hobbled their way toward the star fortress where *Sky Arrow One* was parked.

♠ ♠ ♠

Ace zoomed after the gun wagon. Three blocks later, fresh black tire marks on the cobblestones curved to the right. Ace followed the black arc down a street marked "Indiagade," which headed toward the waterfront.

Ace passed a last few houses. She spotted the water, double pier, and warship. The gun wagon and two hastily placed crates made a ragged barricade at the entrance to the facility. In the midnight gloom, Ace could see one soldier on guard. Others unloaded the truck parked on the pier next to the ship, almost frantic in their haste.

Most disturbingly, Ace could see an inert cloth blob next to the truck. Its outlines resembled a body, and its color was that of Quack's borrowed custodian outfit.

Ace's jaw clenched. She swerved off the road for a moment to wrestle the heavy metal top off a garbage canister. It had two handles, and she positioned it like a shield in one hand and steered the motorcycle with the other. Roaring back into the road, she bore down on the waterfront.

The one soldier at the entrance glanced, then glanced again at the tiny oncoming vehicle. He had trouble interpreting the sight. When one expects a stampede of police cars with lights ablaze and sirens blaring, a single rented motorcycle hardly registers as a threat. Belatedly, he unslung his machine gun.

Ace revved to higher and higher speed on the motorcycle. She peered over the top of her garbage can lid shield to better map the details of the pier layout. The gate guard yelled and opened fire. Ace ducked her head and raised her feet as bullets pinged off the steel lid. She steered by sense of touch, heading for the source of bullets.

The soldier let up on the trigger and leaped sideways, but not soon enough. The impact sent the soldier, motorcycle, shield, and Ace flying. Ace hit the ground on off-balance feet and kicked into a diving forward roll. She found her feet and skidded to a halt. She glanced at the feebly twitching gate guard before chasing her shield, which had rolled ahead.

Shouts rang out, and the pounding of running feet. Ace caught up to the rolling shield, grabbed it, and sprinted on. At her feet, cobblestones gave way to wooden timbers.

Four running shapes converged on her. The nearest shouldered his gun. Ace raised her shield high then slammed it into the ground.

It bounced and rolled like a crazed wheel toward the nearest gunman. He tried to swerve, but he guessed wrong. The metal edge caught him in the stomach and chest with a meaty thud, and he flew backwards to flop boneless on the pier timbers.

Bullets popped and whizzed. Ace veered toward the ship and leaped. She used the chest of the prone gunman as a trampoline to bounce into a dive. Grazing bullets plucked at the tough fabric of her flight suit as she flew through the air. She cleared the edge of the pier by inches, between pier and ship. Her tawny form disappeared below pier level, and there was a splash.

The two downed gunmen stayed down, but three more ran to the edge of the pier and opened fire into the water.

GUY WORTHEY

Chapter 24

As soon as she entered the water, Ace arced her body. Directing her momentum sideways, she veered under the pier. As she broke through the water's surface, the cacophony of gunfire assaulted her ears. She jackknifed up to a barnacle-encrusted crossbeam to observe the fusillade frothing the water for a few moments. Her mouth thinned, and her brows contracted.

The bullets cut off, and shouts rang, "Schnell! Schell! An Bord!"[16]

Ace slid her goggles from her eyes to the top of her cap. They had half filled with water during the short time she was underwater. She unlaced and pulled off her boots and discarded a shredded sleeve. "Quack had better be breathing," she muttered.

Ace slipped back into the water and swam under the pier to its end. As she swam, the gray warship rumbled and screeched. Boilers shot steam to turbines. They spun, transmitting torque through cold gears to the ship's screw. The ship inched forward.

Compared to her worry about Quack, the escaping thieves were secondary. Any gunmen that could walk would be escaping along with their vessel, she reasoned. Ace clambered up on the seaward edge of the pier with haste. If the ship pulled out far enough, she would become visible. Ace scuttled a few paces to

---

[16] "Quickly! Get aboard!"

shelter behind the large truck that had carried the loot from ISPHA to the ship.

"Ciao, signora," came a soft voice.

"Isa?" Ace said, dumbfounded. The brunette photographer rose from behind a crate. With feline grace, she joined Ace beside the truck as the ship glided by on the other side, gradually picking up speed. "What are you doing here?"

Isabella wrung her hands and answered with a question, "Have you seen Charles?"

Ace's brows knit even tighter. "I thought I left you both out of harm's way in the hotel." She glanced at the crumpled heap dressed like a janitor. The body was out in the open, too exposed for Ace at the moment, though the ship would steam out of sight soon.

The warship cleared the end of the dock. As its engine noise declined, a new hum sang in the air. Isabella glanced upwards. With a wry smile, she said, "Your airship, bella."

"Yes," Ace said. "Isa, I have to—"

There was the unmistakable click of the hammer of a pistol. A male voice said, in a British accent, "No sudden moves now. I hate to waste bullets."

Ace had to spin all the way around to find the source of the voice. A blond man sat in the cab of the truck. He grinned like a wolf as he leaned out the window. A small gap separated his upper front teeth. A wicked .45 caliber gun aimed steadily between Ace's eyes.

"You." Ace's teeth set. "What's your game?"

"I wanted you to know who outsmarted who, that's all. Now that you know, goodbye." The wolfish grin deepened. The arm holding the gun extended. The trigger finger tightened.

It was such close range Ace knew her odds were slim. But Ace had never given up before. She wasn't about to start now. Like a startled eel pulling back into its sandy burrow, she ducked.

There was a wicked crack sound. The air by Ace's ear hissed. A burn of gunpowder peppered her ear and the back of her neck.

The *back* of her neck?

Ace fell into a crouch and looked up.

The gap-toothed man in the cab slumped, and his pistol slithered free from nerveless fingers. His shoulder bloomed with a small, red flower. His wolfish grin snapped to a confused scowl. He spluttered, "Scarab? Scarab, what are you d—"

"You talk too much!" Isabella spat back. Then she shot him again.

"Isa!" Ace said, in shock.

"Pah," Isa spat. "He deserved it. So bloodthirsty he is. Was. He did not need to, but he killed the violinists, anyway. And thereby failed. As for you—" Isabella pointed her snub-nose .38 at Ace. "Stand up."

Sluggishly, as if in a dream, Ace straightened. Her jaw sagged open, and her eyebrows worked. Agile her intellect may be, but some twists required more than a moment to sort out. "Why? If you're working for them, why did—"

Isabella glided closer, shaking her head from side to side. "So smart, yet so out of touch."

The dark-haired woman tucked her gun back out of sight in her pocket. Her eyes locked with Ace's. She snaked a hand into Ace's dripping hair and pulled her into a kiss.

♠ ♠ ♠

"Now, go get on your airship and finish what you started, Principessa. I know you will win." Isabella backed away, lips curved ever so slightly in an expression more like triumph than defeat, dark eyes aglow.

Ace stared, mouth slack, lips tingling.

Quack moaned.

Isabella pivoted and whisked toward Copenhagen, soon swallowed by the night.

At the truck, a head and arm dangled motionless from the cab.

Ace shook her head to clear it and pelted over to Quack. She knelt over him, but she didn't spot any bullet holes among his purpling bruises and oozing lacerations.

"Oh, hi, Ace!" Quack managed a small smile, though his rich voice, normally able to fill a theater, barely managed to be heard at all. "Those mercenaries were mad, mad, mad, weren't they?"

"Quack. You're not dead." Ace's throat unclogged, and her voice emerged warm and vibrant.

"It's not for lack of trying. I need to pick my battles better. That was really stupid of me." Quack licked a split lip and winced.

"It's a fine line between foolhardy and brave."

His eyes widened, and he gripped Ace's sleeve. "Ace! The violinist! He's on board the ship!"

CHAPTER 25

"What?" Ace said, unhinged yet again.

"Don't ask me to explain it, but I saw his face. He peeked out from under a tarp as the thugs were laying into me."

Approaching police sirens blended with the hum of *Sky Arrow One*. Ace scanned the now-lonely dock. The two soldiers she had downed lay in heaps, and Isabella had vanished. Ace stood over Quack and waved both hands at the airship. The loose coils of a rope dropped from its gondola. Ace gave the thumbs-up.

She glanced down, her face suddenly hot. "Quack? You didn't, um, didn't *see* anything just now, did you?"

"What do you mean, Ace?" Quack grunted and groaned his way to a sitting position.

"Never mind. I have to go. I hope there's something left of Derkin when we catch up."

Quack didn't bother to reply. A dangling rope danced by, and Ace leapt into the air to snatch it. She glided off over the sea, still wearing her leather helmet but barefoot and ragged.

Gooper and Bert hauled Ace into the gondola. She slapped each of them on the shoulder. "Thanks, fellas.

Quack's all right."

Bert exhaled in a whoosh. "Oh, good."

"But Derkin's aboard the ship."

"Blimey! 'Ow did 'e manage that?" Gooper's bushy red mustache bristled.

Ace said, "I can only guess. Who's in good enough shape to board that vessel?"

"I think I will have to stay here, Lady Ace," Sam said miserably. The archaeologist lay propped up in the lounge with ice bags tied around his knees.

"That seems wise, Sam. Get rifles, Gooper and Bert. There are two or three professional soldiers still able-bodied," Ace said over her shoulder as she scooted toward her cabin.

She popped open her clothes locker and grabbed a spare pair of boots. Dry socks might be nice, too. As she swapped footgear, her glance strayed toward the porthole.

She looked again. A crease formed between her brows as her eyes roved.

Then she saw it. A square area on her desk lay unoccupied. The violin's X-ray had vanished.

In the lounge, Bert tossed a rifle to Gooper. Then his shoulder blades knit together as a cry like an enraged puma ripped from Ace's cabin.

Bert and Gooper dropped into fighting poses, their faces bewildered. The next moment, Ace stalked from her cabin, storms abrew in her eyes. "The X-ray is gone."

Her associates blurted simultaneously, "What?"

"Isa Rosavino, without much doubt. She played a subtle game, but she was working for Dor all along."

Bert's shoulders sagged. "Oh. Oh, no. Not Isa."

Gooper poked him in the ribs. "Rough news, Yank. On the bright side, guv, it explains where yer 'andcuff keys went. Gone in a puff of perfume an' a wink."

Ace's voice sliced like a steel sword. "Talk it over later. Get the ropes and harnesses. We have to drop quickly. They might have searchlights." She raised her voice. "Vivian and Gilbert? Get your pirate hats on. Prepare for boarding."

"Yes, ma'am!" answered Gilbert brightly.

"I see the ship, ma'am," Vivian added. "She's running dark, but the sparks in her funnels give her away."

Halfway down the ropes, dangling exposed over the sea, Gooper rumbled, "That is a monumental hunk of artillery."

"And it's aiming up!" Bert gasped.

"They see us already?" Ace groaned.

The gun dominated the stern of the ship, and its bore was indeed homing in on the airship. Its muzzle flashed. A second later, there was a terrific boom. A massive shell ripped past the dangling trio and beyond the stern of the airship before exploding with another concussion.

"Come on, Vivian! Faster!" Bert urged.

Ace caught sight of movement on the deck next to the gun. A pale face looked up. It was Derkin. Even in the gloom and from a distance, he seemed sick with fear.

The hum of the airship motors deepened.

Smaller muzzle flashes popped as at least two rifles aimed bullets at Gooper, Bert, and Ace.

"Cor! We're sitting ducks 'til—"

The big gun spoke again. The shell screamed through the air, and the concussion rocked *Sky Arrow One* and the three on the ropes. In a bright flash, most of the left-side elevator at the tail of the dirigible shattered into fragments of aluminum.

"She's hit!" bellowed Gooper.

The *Sky Arrow* dipped toward the water and toward the warship. In seconds, the ends of the ropes were dragging in the North Sea, and the boarding party was plummeting toward a splashdown.

Ace gritted her teeth. "This is humiliating. Worst rescue ever."

Bert yelled, "The gun! It's got *Sky Arrow*'s range!"

The cannon raised higher. It seemed inevitable that the next shot would explode inside the dirigible. Ace, Bert, and Gooper dropped below deck level as the *Sky Arrow*'s engines whined a higher note.

Ace caught a last glimpse of Derkin as they descended. Derkin tossed a dark tube into the air. Ace blinked.

"Hold on!" she advised.

There was a boom, as if from a cannon, but it was different. Deeper. And the cannon muzzle didn't flash, but the turret puffed black smoke. *Sky Arrow*'s thrust took effect, and their descent evened out. Ace's feet skittered on the waves.

"Rappel. Now! Full down!" Ace shouted.

"But," Bert objected, then obeyed with alacrity as he understood. The *Sky Arrow* pulled skyward with ever-increasing speed and also drove forward. The ropes sizzled past their metal harness fittings, but even with the brakes off, the three were lifted back into the air, soaring over the deck.

With zing sounds, the ropes left them and twanged off into the air. The three were in free fall. Midair, they studied the smoking hole in the turret of the big gun.

"Wahoooo!" whooped Gooper, wildly windmilling his arms.

The deck rose to meet them, hard. Gooper dropped into a big coil of rope. Bert ripped through the canvas cover of a lifeboat. Ace landed awkwardly on the slopes of a hatch cover and careened off a capstan, undercutting at the knees a mercenary who was trying to aim his gun at her.

"Now, the fun commences," Gooper crowed, gaining his feet only to trip and fall forward after two steps. A bullet whizzed where his body had just been.

Bert poked his head above the gunwale of the lifeboat, smiled woozily, raised his rifle, and snapped off a shot.

"Urk!" cried a voice.

Ace punched her assailant between the legs. He folded. She ripped his gun away and smashed him over the head with it.

Gooper rolled free and headed forward. "Yew got 'im, Bert!" he reported.

Derkin's voice drifted from inside a toppled barrel, "I'm so very glad you are here."

Ace's eyes roved, searching for targets. "We're here, Charles. Glad you're alive."

The violinist crawled out. He had the shakes, but he pulled himself up to wobble on untrustworthy knees. "I don't know how you're not a nervous wreck, Miss

Carroway."

"Good job with that grenade, Charles. We'd be swimming home right about now if you hadn't tossed it."

"If you only knew!" quavered the unsteady man. "I stared at the grenade in my hand an eternity before I worked up the gumption to pull the pin."

"That is the very definition of courage, Charles. Come on, we need to get to the bridge."

"What? Oh, all right. Aiee!" Derkin's eyes flicked up and widened.

Ace dove into the violinist, launching them both sideways. A hail of bullets followed them. Derkin squawked as he was tackled and crushed against the deck. Suddenly, the bullets stopped.

Bert's voice drifted over. "Got him, too." The lawyer emitted a dark chuckle.

"Thanks, Bert!" called Ace. She climbed off Derkin and helped him to his feet.

They skulked forward on the vessel. The shadowy forms of Gooper and Bert paralleled Ace and Derkin. All was quiet except for the chugging of the engines.

A hatch clanked. Gooper, who was nearest, pounced on it. "Ow no, you don't!" His bulging arms flexed and ripped it open. Hands and arms came up with the hatch, gripping the wheel that would have locked it tight. Gooper chortled and made a grab. He seized a wrist and hauled up a wriggling sailor.

Derkin had paused to ogle, but Ace pulled him along. "Come on. Let's leave them to their fun."

As Ace and Derkin scurried on, meaty impacts ended the panicked protests of the hapless sailor.

"Belowdecks we go?" inquired Bert.

"Aye, Bert. Only reg'lar crew left, methinks."

The men's voices faded as Ace and Derkin invaded the bridge. Some of the instruments were aglow, but the bridge was empty of people. Ace crept in, followed by P. Charles Derkin, whose body tremors had abated somewhat.

"Jetzt!"[17] cried a voice. Bodies fell from above. Too late, Ace noticed the hiding places between bulkhead and ceiling in the bridge, and then heavy boots landed on her shoulders. She jackknifed her body and skittered sideways. The off-balance officer thumped awkwardly to the floor. He stuck out an arm to brace himself on the wheelhouse and whipped the other around to point a gun at Ace.

Ace was ready. She pulled the gun arm over her back, and the officer was whirled over and slammed into the floor. Ace fell on him, elbow first. With a grisly pop, his collarbone snapped. The officer curled into a whimpering, ineffective ball.

Ace sprang to her feet to see Derkin imprisoned by a burly arm around his neck. The man in a captain's uniform held Derkin as a human shield between himself and Ace. His service revolver pointed at Derkin's head. He snarled, "Werfe deine Waffe ab!"

Ace reached to her own back, unhooking her heretofore untouched rifle. "Throw down my weapon, you say?" Her golden eyes were those of an eagle, fierce and without pity.

Derkin struggled weakly, clawing at the captain's arm ineffectually. His eyes silently pleaded with Ace.

In a smooth motion, Ace raised her rifle, aimed,

---

[17] "Now!"

and shot, seemingly right at Derkin. Derkin felt a sting at his cheek, as if he had been slapped. The burly arm around his neck relaxed, and the captain fell to the ground. Derkin glanced down. The captain's face below his right eye was a spiderweb tracery of blood.

He stared aghast at Ace. "You ... you ... you shot him? He could have *killed* me!"

Ace studied levers at the helm, deciding which ones to pull. She rattled off distractedly, "Firstly, not likely, psychologically, despite what you see in movies. Secondly, his sidearm was a Sauer 1919, and he still had the safety catch on. An oversight in the heat of the moment, I assume."

The pilot raised her goggles to her forehead and planted fists on her hips, surveying her newly captured domain. The throb of the engines faded to a murmur. The ship lost thrust and coasted forward through the quiet waters.

Derkin felt his cheek. His fingertips came away bloody. "I'm hit," he said faintly.

Suddenly, Ace was there, cradling his head to examine his cheek and ear. "Ah. Some fragments. So sorry. They were mercy bullets. Likely, you'll be feeling sleepy right about now."

"Sleepy?" Derkin repeated. "Oh. Come to think of it, I'm feeling a bit—"

Derkin's world went gray, then black.

CHAPTER 26

Derkin awoke to a curious gentle rocking sensation. His hands fluttered around. By sense of touch, he lay upon a bed, covered with a blanket. His eyes opened. Light streamed in from a square window, but the window frame was aluminum, not wood.

A perfunctory knock at the cabin door announced the arrival of Gilbert. Dressed in his smart white flight suit, he bore a full tray that included a steaming cup and the smell of freshly brewed coffee. "Continental breakfast in bed, sir, compliments of Captain Carroway."

"How lovely." Derkin sat up. He ached. The beginnings of a smile faltered. "Where am I?"

"Over the Øresund Sound, sir, not far from Copenhagen. Captain Carroway is impatient to leave, but there are police ships, at least one fire department ship, and a fair fraction of the Danish Navy."

"So it's over?" Derkin sipped some orange juice.

"Yes, sir. I don't know if you'll get your violin back."

Derkin smirked, then gestured with his fork at Gilbert. "Of all the confusing things I've been through lately, that's one thing I'm sure of. However beautifully it plays, I don't want the deadly thing."

Some days later, Ace and her associates infested the lounge of their New York office. Mrs. Figgins clacked away at typewriter keys nearby.

"Your black eye is all sorts of colors now, Quack," Bert said.

Sam's black mustache seemed to curl in amusement. "Colors vivid enough to inspire Renoir."

"It's all but healed," said Quack. "I'm already itching for the next case."

"I worry about you, sometimes, fellas," Ace drawled. "You're never happy unless you're in dire peril."

"Look 'oo's talkin'," Gooper said.

Ace affected an innocent expression. "I don't go looking for danger. It comes looking for me."

"As if magnetically attracted," Sam said.

"But we're glad it does," Quack said. "We'd be bored, otherwise."

Ace's gold irises defocused. "I can't take a case right now. I have to get a start on the new engine."

"Are you sure?" Mrs. Figgins interjected from afar. "There's a lost kitten on 52nd Avenue."

"I'm sure," said the flyer. "But when I've got a working airplane, I know what's next."

Sam said, "What, Lady Ace?"

"Find Darko Dor." The gleam of the hunt sparked in her eye. "And bring him to justice."

The men sat up straight, and grins broke out.

"Wicked good," said Bert.

"By thunder, I'm in," said Quack.

"An exquisite proposition, ma'am."

"Music to my ears, memsahib."

Ace scanned the row of eager faces, and a lump formed in her throat. Her voice came thick. "You fellas are the best." Her eyes flicked to the fleecy clouds visible through the windows. The sky called to her, as it had all her days. "I'd better scoot off to Lark Haven, but you fellas get down to the Office of Naval Intelligence and see what they can dig up on an operative with the code name *Mongoose*. It's a name Derkin overheard from Isabella."

Quack said, "Can do, Ace."

Bert sighed. "I can't believe Isa was working for Dor."

Sam stamped his cane on the floor. "And she stole the plans for the new engine. Along with Darko Dor, we should stop Isabella Rosavino."

Ace cleared her throat. "Um. I didn't tell you this before, but ... she saved my life. She shot her fellow agent Tim just before *he* shot *me*."

Four pairs of eyes stared. Ace's face slowly colored from gold to a deeper bronze.

The office door slammed open, and a lanky figure in a Stetson and cowboy boots strode in, bowlegged. He ducked to clear the doorframe.

"Blimey. Not 'im." Gooper's mustache drooped.

Sam waved his cane energetically. "Tombstone!"

The incoming buckaroo flapped a hand. "Howdy there, fellers. Howdy, Ace, ma'am." He grinned. "What'd I miss?"

Ballycrispin Crier

Cork County Daily Wednesday, Sept 13, 1922

BLUEBEARD EXECUTED

VERSAILLES, Sep. 12 — "Bluebeard" Henri Landru, the most infamous criminal of modern times, was executed on the guillotine early yesterday, for the murder of ten women and one boy. A large crowd, which was kept in check by 400 cavalrymen, turned out before daylight to witness the execution which took place in the street in the center of the city. Landru, who up to the last day had expected a reprieve, met death stoically. He refused any religious consolation. Just before he was summoned to take his place on the guillotine, he said "I am innocent. I have nothing to add."

Henri Desire Landru, "The Bluebeard of Gambals," was arrested on Oct 4, 1919, charged with the murder of the women, some of them wealthy and foolish widows, and all possessing property, whom he lured to his villa on the outskirts of Paris with promises of marriage, only to kill them to secure their savings.

From the time of his arrest up until his trial, which began Mar 7, 1922, before the Versailles assizes, and ended May 30, "Bluebeard" was engaged in answering or evading questions of the police, the investigating magistrate, and other court officials. He proved a most stubborn prisoner, and preserved an astonishing nonchalance almost up to the moment of his conviction.

An absolute lack of proof that the "missing" women were dead constituted the backbone of his defense. After his arrest the house he rented at Gambals was ransacked and almost destroyed in a search for the remains of the missing

AIRSHIP PLAGUE CONTINUES

GLOUNSHAROON. Sep. 12 — Local fisherman Conall Flanagan told his first true story yesterday, though it seemed wilder than his usual blarney at first. Spies dressed in black, said the stalwart, exchanged places between a silver airship and a sleek yacht, both of which vessels had intruded upon Flanagan's fishing waters. Both spies were women, he reported, of youthful vigor.

The wire service confirmed parts of his story, dealing a blow to local skeptics. An airship landed in Plymouth, England on the same day that Flanagan spotted it. It was the SKY ARROW ONE, built by Carroway Aeronautics of Lark Haven, Pennsylvania, United States. No doubt Captain Cecilia "Ace" Carroway herself was aboard.

The airship last passed over Cork County in July, as reported by dog trainer Derry Witherspoon, in connection with a Devonshire jewel heist. Carroway and crew recovered the stolen jewels.

This time, it appears that Carroway was busy rescuing kidnapped violinist P. Charles Derkin of Toronto and his violin. The yacht had been used to whisk the violinist overseas, the dastardly deed performed by unidentified criminals. Details on how Carroway commandeered the yacht remain unclear, but Derkin's status is reported as alive, well, and free.

It seems that Ace Carroway is determined to perform rescues and recover stolen items, and that these activities frequently force her to fly over Cork County. Keep a sharp eye out, lads and lasses, and you, too might spot a silvery dirigible lettered with NX51 on the side.

NOTES

Dear reader, I do hope you enjoyed this installment in the *Adventures of Ace Carroway*. Here at the end, please allow me a few moments to sort reality from fiction.

Cremona, Italy, around 1700 was home to two families of violin makers (luthiers) whose names you might have heard of: Stradivari and Guarneri. The modern violin had been around more than a century, but these craftsmen invented subtle changes that elevated violin-making to an art form. Amazingly, many of the violins, violas, and cellos crafted in Cremona are still played and are still among the highest-quality instruments ever made. Most fetch jaw-dropping prices on the rare occasions they come up for sale.

The virtuoso violinist Niccolò Paganini (1782-1840) owned a Stradivari-made violin famed for its volume and expressiveness. Its nickname was *Il Canone* in Italian, or *The Cannon* in English. Today, that violin is a national treasure, kept much of the time in a museum. On the special occasions that *Il Canone* is handled and played (always by a world-renowned musician, naturally), it is accompanied by armed guards and a heavy safe for storage. My fictional version of "the Cremona Cannon" is but a tiny departure from reality.

As for Ace, she'll need tungsten, molybdenum, and titanium for her new engine, and that will lead her to Alaska's inside passage. There she sees an impossible sight, and her next chilling and twisted adventure is entitled *Ace Carroway and the Ghost Liner*.

ABOUT THE AUTHOR

Wyoming native Guy Worthey traded spurs and lassos for telescopes and computers when he decided to pursue astrophysics. Whenever he temporarily escapes the gravitational pull of stars and galaxies, he writes fiction, now in the slightly less rectangular state of Washington. He plays jazz bass and happily stretches genre boundaries to find common musical ground with his classical violinist wife Diane. A beacon of inclusivity in a fractured world, he likes both cats and dogs. Creamed eggs on toast is the earthy name of his favorite food, but once in a while, he samples the celestial delights of chocolate.

ACKNOWLEDGMENTS

Especial thanks to my editors, Sonya and Heather. Love and gratefulness to my family, for they are a wellspring of support that never runs dry.

THE ADVENTURES OF ACE CARROWAY

guyworthey.net

www.ingramcontent.com/pod-product-compliance
Lightning Source LLC
Chambersburg PA
CBHW071246130626
46556CB00003B/1191